Great Minds Die Alike

By Stephen Boudreaux

To My Little Buddy and the Water

Contents

Chapter 1 – In the Beginning

God created the Heavens and the Earth. The Earth He called His vineyard. Some parts of that vineyard were made up of good ground, with luscious fields fed by cold clear waters racing down in torrents from distant mountains. God was pleased with this part of His vineyard, and man rejoiced in the bounty there.

Another part of the vineyard was not so pleasant. There were many trees in the low country, near the delta of a large river which flowed into the great waters. But there was too much water, and it moved slowly. It was not clear fresh mountain water. It was brown and brackish. And God blessed the delta and gave it fish and big birds, snakes and alligators, frogs and bugs.

The delta, though poor, became God's special place. He knew that when man lived there, he would be strong and mighty. Not mighty in war, but in survival. Man would love the land and take care of God's special ground. He made it harsh to keep out those who would not appreciate it.

The creatures living there would afflict and torment man, but they became nourishment to those who called this part of the vineyard home. Those whom God allowed to live there gave thanks.

They lived on the water or found some dry ground to build houses. They suffered heat and oppressive humidity. The great winds blew from the east and rained havoc on the delta. But it was not a punishment from God, it was just a test to prove man worthy.

Man stayed.

And God was well-pleased.

Chapter 2 – Snake Girl

Roxanne Cormier dit Boucher never tired of her father Remy's account of the Creation. She knew it was a little skewed due to his love for the bayous where they lived, but Roxie, as her friends called her, rejoiced in the bayou region of Louisiana.

Lisette and Remy Cormier dit Boucher were born and raised in the bayous. They grew up on Cajun food and Zydeco. They wanted for nothing. The bayou gave them food and shelter. They were also close enough to civilization to have electricity and some of the small necessities of life, fit for raising a daughter.

Roxie became the spitting image of her mother: feisty with long jet-black hair and deep dark eyes. She inherited her *joie de vivre* from her loving parents, a trait that helped her through the death of her mother, who fell ill to some virus that may have crept in from the more modern civilization.

Roxie had to handle the deep sorrow that Remy felt for the loss of his wife. But the two vowed to push on. Remy had a child to raise, to teach, to show respect for the land and the slow water, and to grow to be a woman like his Lisette.

Roxie went to school and excelled in all the basics of learning. She was never sick, never late for school, never caused trouble with the other children, although sometimes her accent got in the way, but it was the bayou. People just talk different there. Don't mean they're ignorant, but time on the water taught Roxie more than school ever could.

Remy knew every waterway and bayou, every person in the area. He could tell stories, albeit exaggerated sometimes, of the people who lived nearby. Roxie took notes on all he told her: how gators stay warm in the winter, how the herons hunt for fish, which snakes were poisonous, and which were not, how to catch crawfish, and especially, how to cook. Just because life was simple, didn't mean their food had to be.

Remy worked the swamp tours, which brought in enough money to get things the bayou didn't provide. He always had enough for his daughter to dress like a lady when she went to school or church on Sunday, and of course, there were the more vital items of clothing: waders and muck boots, plus the necessary fishing gear.

Didn't bother Remy if the Northerners laughed at his accent or what he wore. It was part of the whole act. *If these Yankees wanna see a show, we give it to them.*

Then he would just steer up to a gator sitting quietly in the water, toss a piece of chicken in when the tourists were gawking elsewhere. That old gator would make such a fuss and splash. Tourists would scramble trying to move to the other side of the tour boat.

If the bayous ever drained out, locals would find plenty of cameras stuck in the mud from all those folks from the North losing their stuff over the side. Some tried to give the tour managers grief over losing their precious Nikons because of the tour guide. The manager just pointed to a sign on the wall.

> *We ain't responsible for the loss of your belongings. If you wish to go in the water and find the lost item yourself, we'll be glad to take you back up the bayou at no charge.*

Funny thing, no one ever took them up on the offer.

In the summers when Roxie was not in school, she was a deckhand, handling the mooring lines, directing tourists, taking pictures, feeding gators. Remy was proud of his daughter and made sure tour management compensated her accordingly. She was a hit. People left comments about the "Bayou Girl". It always helped business.

Even when some New York City kid thought he could show how tough he was. Roxie was not tall or muscular, but she could see trouble coming. This kid was spouting how cool he was that if he saw a gator, he could punch one in the face. It was annoying the other guests. And he was chiding Roxie.

"You're just a girl," the kid taunted. "You couldn't make it in the streets of Brooklyn. They'd eat you alive."

Remy knew his daughter was getting a little uneasy, but he had to focus on steering the tour boat and pointing out the usual sights on the bayou.

Roxie said nothing, just motioned to her father to slide along that rock near the bank. A wry smile came over Remy as he pulled the boat close to a cypress on the water's edge.

Roxie slowly walked over to the starboard side of the boat, slid on her gloves, and scooped up a black snake resting on a log. She spun around holding the snake and shoved it toward the bully. The kid screamed like a little girl, wet his pants, and ran toward the bow where his parents were sitting.

The whole tour group laughed, even the parents. Cameras went clicking all over capturing this young girl holding up a black snake. Knowing that their child was in the wrong and were in no condition to defend him for his annoying behavior, the parents said, "You made your bed."

Roxie leaned back over the side and carefully set the snake down. With his 15 seconds of fame complete, the snake slithered off to safer places. She walked up to the embarrassed kid, who had tears in his eyes and a light jacket around his waist so as not to show his soaked pants.

"No, sir," she said to the kid. "I don't suppose I could make it on your streets back home." She took off her glove and extended her hand as a gesture of Southern politeness.

The kid replied, "You're crazy. I'm not touching you," thinking she would pull some other embarrassing stunt.

Roxie pulled back her hand, replaced her glove, and went back to stand by her father who was doing everything he could to keep from laughing out loud. *Yankees*, she whispered, shaking her head.

News got back to the tour manager. After the group was gone, he called her over.

"Miss Roxie, this is a reputable business we have here. Scaring the customers ain't in the brochures."

"Mr. Zeb," she replied. "I apologize, but he was making—"

"Go no further, little lady. The rest of the group was in an uproar." Zeb's big old belly shook while he laughed. "Some said stuff like that should be part of the tour."

A smile came over Roxie delighted to please the management. "Well, Sir. I wanted to toss the peeshwank into the bayou, and let the gators get him."

"I must say. For a young lady, you got a bit of cayenne in you."

"Maybe, Sir, but they need to respect this place. Don't come down here showing your city boy face to me."

"I think Pere Remy put a cunja on him," Old Zeb said laughing. Cunja was a curse. No one wanted that.

"Papa would've done that for sure. and I promise you, I'll be nicer to the guests."

"Well, Sha, you a star. Some Yank with a polaroid captured you and the snake," Zeb smiled, showing her the photograph. "We'll just put it up right here on the board. People see it, they gonna want more of that action."

"I think I scared that poor snake. He was just sunning himself. Then suddenly, he was front row circus."

"That he was, Sha. That he was."

A few weeks later, the kid from New York sent the swamp tour manager a letter apologizing for his rude behavior. His parents probably put him up to it. He wanted to pass on to the "Snake Girl" that any time she wanted to come to New York, he would show her around.

The manager passed the letter on to Roxie. She smiled and told her father. "I have the cypress. Don't need the tall buildings and millions of people."

Crumpling the letter, she tossed it in the trash and went on about her cleaning the tour boat in preparation for the next group of tourists from places far away.

"Rochie, there's a wonderful world out there with wonderful sights and good people, good food, good music," said Remy. "You can't stay here your whole life."

"Oui, Papa. One day," Roxie said.

"That's my girl. Just leave them snakes down here, though."

"Now, now, Papa," she said laughing. "We don't wanna scare the snakes."

Chapter 3 – Eugenie Douillard

"Rochie! Come on, Cher. Monsieur Soleil ain't waiting for us. Hurry along," Pere Remy yelled as he put the last of the supplies into his pirogue.

"Coming, Papa," Roxie replied. "Just getting my journal."

She knew best not to make her father wait. She also knew that it was eight in the morning. The sun was still north of due east in the middle of June. There was plenty of sun time left. Yet her respect and love for father caused celestial movement to take second place.

As Roxie jumped into the pirogue, Remy noticed his daughter was out of breath. "No need to hurry, ma fille. You know I was funnin' ya. Ready for more exploring?"

"Oui, Papa," she replied. "Where to this morning?"

"How about we go to Bayou Piquant."

"You just want to visit that Miss Douillard," she said smiling.

Remy smiled back. "I'm bringing her some honey from that place south the Air Force Base. See here?"

Remy pulled back a tarp revealing 4 mason jars filled with liquid gold.

"She will love you even more, that Miss Douillard will."

Replacing the tarp, Remy replied with a sigh. "She's been secluded out on Bayou Chevreuil. Be nice to cheer her up."

"Be nice to get her famous brown bread, you mean," replied Roxie.

Remy made no reply, but the shy grin spoke volumes. "You're a good man, Papa. Mama is proud watching down from above."

"Your mother has better things to do up there," pointing to the sky and looking up, "than be watching us exploring places no one wants to visit."

"That's why you have me," said Roxie. "To keep you on the water."

"And to keep you out of trouble," replied Remy.

"You're funning me again," Roxie said laughing. "You know I'm a good girl."

"Okay, good girl. Get that bow line undone and we'll be off."

"Aye, Captain," Roxie said with a good nautical salute.

Tossing the line into the pirogue, Remy yanked the starting rope on the outboard motor. Rochelle and Remy Cormier dit Boucher were off on another adventure.

The bayou is hot in June. The humidity so thick you need a machete and lots of bugspray. Remy preferred garlic. Seems like mosquitos have a repulsion to the magical cloves. Maybe that was why people wore garlic around their necks to ward off werewolves. Where the two were going, though, there were no werewolves. Just moccasins, gators, and other more dangerous fauna that cared not about garlic.

If anyone has ever been in the bayous, it is a place you don't want to go if you don't want to get lost. It is a place where the air is heavy, the trees confuse you, the water is not blue. More like a coffee color. It is not the glamorous waterway as seen from the camera view in the movies. If you know the bayou, it lets you live. Otherwise it will let you die.

The pirogue set off up Bayou L'Ours past Zeb's Swamp Tours, a place where city folk go to get an air boat ride into a world far from Rodeo Drive and the Magnificent Mile. Sometimes Roxie wished she were in an air boat. At least the trip would be shorter, but she would miss the sounds of life that existed in the back waters. Remy didn't need anything but his faithful pirogue, a trusty outboard, a few landmarks, and of course, a loaded Winchester. Just in case something got hungry.

Roxie took copious notes. Even though she had been up this bayou many times, there was always a feature she missed, some different kind of cypress, some new outcropping, or some new place to dock. Every new trip she brought out a new notebook with date and location labeled. She drew, annotated, collected, pasted.

"How far is Bayou Piquant, Papa?" she asked interrupting her writing and Remy's humming.

"Couple miles, not as the crow flies. First Bayou Boeuf, into Lac des Allemands, then into Bayou Chevreuil. Why, Rochie? You bored?"

"Mais non, Papa. I just didn't want to miss anything."

"You keep writing, you'll miss it all, Cher."

"Helps me remember, Papa."

"You, young ones. I know every bayou in this area, because I use my eyes, and nose. I remember because my eyes do the writing and my brain is my notebook."

Remy was not chastising his daughter. It was simply a teaching moment.

"I'm thirteen," she replied.

"Cher, when I was your age—"

Roxie finished imitating her father. "I could find Bayou Gauche from Bayou Black with my eyes closed. I know, but only because you had the intracoastal to help you."

"Because I chose to see." Remy smiled at his daughter, reached over the side, and flung some water at her.

"Hey, watch the notebook. You'll get it wet." She returned the gesture to Remy.

Then with a serious look, Remy said, "Rochie, how about we do this. You up for an adventure?"

Puzzled, Roxie replied, "Of course, Papa. What?"

Remy reached out and took the notebook from her hand and placed it gently under the tarp with the jars of honey.

"Rochie, on this trip, we do it my way. We write with our eyes."

Recognizing that her normal means of "remembering" was getting put on hold, she replied, "You win, but—"

"I dislike buts. What're you thinking?"

"When we get to Miss Douillard's, you have to tell her you like her."

With a frown, Remy replied, "For thirteen, you seem to know too much about affections."

"Sometimes I see more than I write, Papa. I know you have feelings for her, or else," Roxie said pointing to the honey. "You wouldn't come all the way out here just to drop this off."

Remy leaned back a little in a contemplative stance. He knew his daughter was growing up, that there were things that he could not provide for her, that she could use a woman's nurture to provide those "finishing touches" every girl needs to become a woman.

"Papa?" she asked, thinking she struck a nerve.

Remy leaned forward elbow on knee, Roxie mimicked the positioning.

"I only have to say I like her, no? That was your 'but'?"

"Well, I was hoping for a little more show of affection, but yes, Papa."

Relieved, Remy sat back again and said "D'accord."

Roxie, out of respect for her father and the conditions he proposed, set her pen down, scooted to the bow, and faced forward.

"Okay, Papa. Teach me."

"I'm not here to teach you. Just keep your eyes open and remember everything you hear, see, smell, and feel. Let the bayou teach you. Respect her and she will reward you."

Roxie did not reply. Remy did not need a response from her. He saw her lean forward with hands on the bow, take deep breaths, and move her head side to side. He noticed her take in the bayou, the water, the trees, the sounds of birds, the molasses-like air. It filled her notebook of memories more than a pen could attempt to do.

Time disappeared. Even though the sun moved across the sky and heated the air even more and brought new shadows and lighting to the water, Roxie watched. Her father hummed, but the soft music didn't interfere. She saw every tree, every open field along the water, incoming tributaries beckoning "Come visit me next time."

The stale air did not distract, although a rogue bug would get in the way or a mosquito would try to get through the garlic fortress. Roxie felt the bends in the water, the turns that shifted shadows in the pirogue. Occasionally, Remy would interrupt the silence with some tidbit of nautical landmark. Roxie would simple reply. "Yes, I see."

She may have already noticed or not. It didn't matter. Any additional input from Remy was welcoming and almost a verbal sign that he was in the back steering.

Closing in on a small channel from the left, Roxie heard a dog barking. "Miss Douillard's cul-de-sac coming up," Roxie said.

Remy laughed at her use of cul-de-sac. As he steered down the channel, the dog stood at the end of dock barking madly. It was an old heeler, not used to visitors, it seems. No wonder. Not many people come by.

"Hush, Pepin," Remy yelled as they approached the dock.

Pepin, the dog stopped barking immediately and stood still, tail wagging furiously. As Remy cut the engine and the pirogue glided softly to dock, Roxie jumped out with line in hand and secured the boat to the cleats.

"Good dog," she said as he came up and licked her face.

"Pepin. Watch your manners," came a voice shouting from beyond the dock.

Eugenie Douillard hurried out toward visitors. She was a petite woman, dressed in a long cotton skirt, swamp boots and long sleeve shirt. She waved to Remy and Roxie. A broad smile came across her face, glad to see another human and relieved to talk to someone else besides Pepin.

"My, my, Cher." Eugenie said to Roxie. "Such a lovely young lady. Why are you here with this old geezer?" she said laughing.

"Old you say?" replied Remy. "Maybe I will take my jars of honey elsewhere, Miss Douillard."

"Best you apologize, Miss Douillard, if you know what is good for you," said Roxie. "And thank you for the compliment."

Seeing Remy pulling back the tarp revealing the golden treasure lying underneath, Eugenie replied in surprise.

"Oh, my. Monsieur Cormier. I am so sorry," Eugenie said humbly. "You do know how to make an old woman feel good."

"Old you say?" replied Remy. "Miss Douillard, you shall outlive us all. Good Lord knows they ain't enough bayou in Heaven to handle you."

"Call me Eugenie, please, Remy. At our age, it is proper that first names are sufficient. Beside fifty ain't old. Just seasoned, shall we say."

Eugenie walked out on the dock and gave a Roxie a hug. "You are just as lovely as your mother. God rest her soul."

"Thank you, Miss Douillard. And you are as spry as ever," Roxie replied, kissing Eugenie on the cheek.

"What do you think of the little present?"

"Well, your father is not little."

Eugenie and Roxie laughed. Remy turned a few shades of blush. He was not little. A tall drink of water. Slender but strong, with lower forearms like Popeye's from many years of steering up and down the bayous and spending time in a crew on sailboats taking deliveries for rich people who didn't want to sail their 46' Beneteau from Annapolis to the Gulf. They preferred to let some deck hand do the work, and they could relax on the calm waters of the Gulf after a short plane trip. Remy and his health should last for another few decades.

Roxie hoped that he would spend the rest of those years with someone his age. Someone like Miss Eugenie Douillard. They would be happy on the bayou, especially after Roxie went off to school and acquired her own life.

"I think she was talking about the honey, Miss Eugenie," said Remy.

"Whatever you want to think, Remy," replied Eugenie. "Now bring that stuff inside and we can spend some time catching up with the real world."

"We would love to stay, but we have to get to Bayou Piquant before sunset."

"Bayou Piquant! Lordy." Eugenie exclaimed. "Ain't nothin' up there. Ain't more than a few miles. You're not boating all the way to Vacherie. At least come in. Refresh yourself. Let your lovely daughter here set a spell."

"I could use the cahbin, Miss Douillard." Roxie said. "I have been holding it in."

"Rochie, you should have said something." Remy replied, feeling somewhat inattentive to his daughter's needs.

"I didn't want us to stop, knowing that Miss Douillard was nearby."

"Eugenie, please. Call me Eugenie."

"Miss Douillard will be fine for now." Remy chimed in. "Out of respect, you know."

"Remy, you are a gentleman. Now come in for a little while, and then I will scoot you two on your way."

"Much obliged, Eugenie." Remy said with a bow.

"Pepin, allons." Roxie said, and the dog followed her into the house.

Eugenie Douillard had a humble home, back in the trees. Not much breeze but the canopy shielded the hot sun except for later in the summer evenings. There were plenty of fans going to circulate the thick air with enough airflow to make life comfortable.

Eugenie was a widow, like Remy, though single much longer. After her husband died from becoming alligator meal, she chose to stay in the bayou. Her only son left for more populous places northward. Before he left, however, he rigged the home with enough solar panels to keep the place lighted. The stove ran on propane. Eugenie lived a simple life, not wanting for anything. Visits from Remy were a bonus that delighted her. Not to mention the honey.

The visitors' stay was not lengthy, enough to deliver the gold in a jar and catch up with some of the news of the area and the people. It was enough for Remy and Eugenie. Well, maybe the latter would have preferred longer visits, but Roxie was there, and they were on a mission of discovery.

Roxie enjoyed being at the Douillard home. It was good for Eugenie and Roxie to have some girl time, some bonding, and despite the simple living conditions, Eugenie was a lady. Remy took advantage of that attribute and welcomed any sort of teaching moment for his daughter.

Chapter Four – The Moccasin

Life was good. Remy steered the pirogue. Roxie sat at the bow, listening to the soft hum of the outboard and the birds and insects singing, trying to feel for any breeze that would bless their moment.

"Rochie, what you think of this part of the bayou?" Remy asked, his words startling her, interrupting her concentration.

"Looks the same as every other part of the bayou. Am I supposed to be seeing something else?"

"No, Cher. You're seeing it right. We go miles and miles. Nothing much changes. Shadows are only things changing round here."

"Then how do you find your way back?" she asked inquisitively.

"Well, you pick one tree that looks different and you remember something about it," he said. "When you saw

Auntie Hazel at the last family reunion, what do you remember?"

Roxie giggled. "That mole on her face, Papa. She may wear a different dress every day, but that mole gives her away."

"Always something different about that one thing midst all these trees, bushes and such. See that cypress there?"

"Which one? I see so many."

"That's right. Now pick one that is different."

Roxie scrutinized each tree. "That one, Papa," she said pointing to one off the port side. "That big growth just above the waterline."

"Any other tree got that?"

"Maybe someplace else, but I don't see any around here."

"Then at this place, we call it Auntie Hazel's Mole. Give these landmarks a name you don't forget. You come down here on your own, you start seeing all sorts of landmarks."

"You have names for yours, Papa?"

"Mais oui, Cher. See that stump sticking out of the water?"

"Sure do."

"Looks like a coon head. That's the name I gave it. We're going past Coon Head Alley."

Roxie and Remy laughed, looking for other interesting "landmarks".

"Okay, my turn," Roxie said scanning. "See all that moss hanging from the tree? We'll call that old Sam's Beard."

"Coo, Cher, good one."

"I guess you could spend your whole life on the bayou and not name everything."

"I suppose. Only name what you need to get home. Otherwise your brain fills up with gumbo."

"Yeah, but how do you know things like Coon Head will be there next time you need it?"

"You don't. You come up here after a big hurricane. Shoot, who knows what survives?"

"I understand that, Papa. Can we stop over at this grassy area? Nature is calling again, and I need to answer."

"Bien sur," said Remy as he steered the boat onto the shore enough for Roxie to climb over the bow.

"I'll hurry, Papa."

"Take ya time, ma fille. I'll just be tuning up this motor for the trip back."

Remy turned off the outboard and hopped out. He pulled the boat more onto shore. As he reached into the water to pull the engine up, a water moccasin came around the opposite side of the boat. Remy didn't see it. The snake lunged out at Remy and struck his left arm above the wrist, and he jerked back and ripped the snake off his arm.

"Rochie," Remy said shouting.

Roxie replied from beyond the trees. "Just a second, Papa."

"Rochie! We need to go now."

Roxie heard a different tone in her father's voice. "Coming."

She hurried back to the boat to see her father on the ground lying next to the pirogue.

"Papa, you okay?" she asked.

"Moccasin decided he wanted to introduce his self," he said showing Roxie the blood on his arm. "We need to get back to Miss Douillard's place now."

"Let me help you into the boat."

"I can get it. You just get the motor started and head back. I will sit up and relax. Don't want the venom going through me too quickly, now."

"Yes, Papa."

Roxie helped her father into the boat and started the outboard. She pushed the bow back into the water and climbed in.

"You know how to get back?" Remy asked.

"I think so. But you can help me, right?"

"Bien sur, Cher. Just remember what you saw coming up here."

"Past Coon Head and then Auntie Hazel."

Remy's throat started to close, and he had a hard time breathing or swallowing. "We gotta call for help, Rochie. You just hurry as fast as you can."

"Papa, how you gonna call anyone? We have no phone."

"Just get back to Miss Douillard and mind the turns. Old Winchester gonna make a call for us," he said, barely whispering the words.

Remy took the shotgun and struggled to load rounds. He fired up in the air, startling Roxie, making her hold her ears. Roxie watched her father from the back of the boat. She knew sounds like that would bring others out from nowhere to find them.

Remy continued to struggle with his breathing, firing more warning shots as Roxie opened the throttle as wide as she could. Panic set in, and Remy stopped moving. He slumped forward resting on the butt of the shotgun.

Roxie cried shouting. "Papa, Papa. Help. Help. Anyone."

In all the confusion, Roxie realized that that bayou and shadows and landmarks had all changed, and she motored down the wrong channel. The sun changed its position and the shadows. She could not find her place on the water.

"Papa, you okay? Papa?"

She ran the boat up on a nearby bank and maneuvered to the front, grabbing Remy's shoulders, and moved him back. She saw emptiness in her father's eyes, partly closed, his mouth open, not breathing.

Roxie screamed. "Papa, no. Papa. Help."

She got out of the boat with the shotgun, loaded more shells, and started firing frantically. Then from the distance, she heard a power boat with large engines. She kept firing.

Turning into her channel, she saw two men, one at the helm, the other at the bow holding a rifle, as if he were coming up on poachers. Roxie dropped the gun and ran toward the shore. screaming and waving her hands.

"Over here. come help. Papa's been bit and he ain't breathing."

Arnie Hooker, the man at the bow yelled out to the girl. "Roxie? Arnie here. What's wrong with your daddy?"

"He was bit. I tried to get back, but I made the wrong turn and got lost."

"Damn, child. You did the right thing, firing that gun of his. Now hop on. Buster and I, we get your daddy in." Arnie and Buster pulled Remy into their boat leaving the pirogue and belongings on the bank. They reversed engines and took off for town.

Arnie got on the CB radio. "Mayday. Mayday. We need a landline hop. Come on back."

Voice on the CB. "Arnie, that you? Wassup?"

"Old Remy Cormier. Bit by a moccasin. Looks bad. We headin' to Bayou L'Ours where it crosses 307. Get Doc Ribeau there now."

"Damn. We on it. Punch that boat."

"We're flying. His daughter is with us. She in hysterics."

"That was what we heard? Gunshots getting our attention?"

"Yeah, buddy. We was coming down from Vacherie when we heard the shots. Figured some poachers was bagging gators again."

"Damn poachers. What's your twenty?"

"We just got onto the lac. Bayou Boeuf just ahead."

"Damn, boy. You are hauling."

"Remy one of us, son. He need us to move."

"We got the call in. Doc Ribeau is standing by. Pull up to the swamp tours dock. We let them know you was coming."

"10-4. Much obliged. Thanks for the hop."

"Is what we do out here. You give us a shout back when you find out about old Remy."

"We will, buddy."

"Tell Miss Roxie, she be okay. Doc will fix up her daddy."

Roxie heard the show of concern from the CB and looked up at buster driving. "Will Papa be okay? He isn't moving."

"Don't worry yourself none, child. Old Remy is tough as these bayous. No moccasin gonna beat him. Your papa knows best to relax. Don't let that venom spread."

Roxie could not share the same feeling. She considered her father's eyes and knew he was no longer there. She was not familiar with dying. Maybe she did have a glimmer of hope that he would pull through. She didn't realize that the bayou was teaching her something else about life. And the end of it.

At the swamp tours dock, Arnie yelled to someone standing at the dock. "Hey, catch this line."

Doc Ribeau stood there as the boat was tied up. "Get him up here quick as you can. I've got some antivenin, and an ambulance just happened to be in the area. We're going to St. Anne's, twenty minutes away."

Arnie and another person helped the lifeless Remy into the back of the ambulance. Roxie climbed in, and the doors closed.

Chapter 5 – The Hospital

Eugenie Douillard hurried into the hospital waiting room. Roxie sat in a chair in the corner, knees up to her chin. When she noticed Eugenie come in, she started crying and ran to up to her old friend. Eugenie wrapped her arms around the sobbing girl.

"Oh, Miss Eugenie, he's gone. Papa's gone," Roxie cried.

"I'm so, so sorry, child. I got here as soon as I could," Eugenie replied. "I heard the chatter on the CB and knew something wasn't right."

"Bayou killed him, Miss Eugenie."

"Poor thing, poor Miss Roxie. No bayou killed him. Was a snake."

"Same thing," burying her head into the saddened woman.

"Your daddy lived the bayou, my dear. He was a part of it. Just one of those happenings only God knows the answers to."

"Momma's long gone, now Papa. All I have left is you."

"You sure do, Cher. You sure do. But life is giving you another turn like a new bayou all to yourself."

"I don't know any other life, Miss Eugenie."

"I hope you don't mind, but I thought it wise and proper and all, to call your brother and tell him."

Roxie stepped back from Eugenie as tears flowed down her face.

"I can't live with him. He's a city boy now. He has a family of his own. Doesn't want his little sister tagging along."

"You may think that now, but he is family. He can provide things for your future, that I can't at this moment."

"You know I will do fine with you and Pepin."

"For some things, fine works. Other things require more than just an old woman and a dog and the backwater. You need good education, and another view of life than us people on the bayou. Away from gators, mudbugs, snakes, mosquitos the size of crows."

"All I want is Papa."

"Cher, he's not gone. Body maybe, but all those times with you and him on the water. They're not gone. Keep those memories."

"And what about the memory of getting lost and not getting Papa help in time?"

"Some memories haunt us. I must tell you, child you will never lose those moments. Whether they be wonderous or horrifying. The good thoughts will enlighten your soul, the bad ones well, they be like a cunja."

Roxie kept quiet and sat back in the chair, staring into some place far away. Eugenie let her have some time to process her future.

"When is Paul coming?"

"He'll be here in the morning."

"What about the funeral?"

"About time we set down and discussed it. Never thought I would have to do that with a thirteen-year old."

"Cremation. Ashes on Bayou Piquant."

"Think Paul should have a say in that?"

"I don't care what he thinks."

"Now, Miss Roxanne. Family respect."

Roxie looks up eyes full of tears ready to spill. "I'm sorry, Miss Douillard." Roxie straightened up with a more businesslike countenance. "I shall strongly recommend to my brother the proper course of action for our father's funeral."

"You shall be a lady in no time."

Roxie said to herself, *Screw them all.*

Chapter Six – An Empty Pirogue

Ten power boats and one pirogue gathered at the inlet of Bayou Piquant. The pirogue belonged to Remy. It was towed out by the lead boat. The others followed solemnly behind. Arnie was at the helm of the lead boat, and Roxie stood alongside him holding an urn with her brother Paul behind her.

Eugenie Douillard sat in the second boat captained by Buster. Other friends occupied the other crafts. There was no minister. Paul spoke loud enough for all to hear. "I want to thank y'all for taking time to come to be with me and my sister Roxanne. I know he was loved by everyone here, and I know this was where he wanted his ashes to be spread."

Roxie muttered to herself. *You didn't know anything about where he wanted to be.*

Paul continued. "The bayou was his life. Let the bayou receive him now."

Muffled "Amens" whispered out over the still water. Roxie took the urn, and opened the lid pouring the ashes out over the brown water. Arnie untied the pirogue, and with a long pole, pointed the empty craft toward the bank. Slowly the boat stopped and came to rest in the black mud.

Eugenie pushed back the tears for a special friend, and with a sad smile she proclaimed, "Laissez les bon temps rouler. We have fais do-do."

The whole crowd whooped and hollered followed, by a symphony of boat horns trumpeting a new addition to Kingdom Come.

Buster in a soft voice, spoke toward the young girl next to him. "May the good Lord give Remy his own bayou up there."

The procession turned around heading back home.

Roxie on seeing the grounded pirogue pass by muttered, *Never again, Papa*. Never again would she get lost, in honor of her father.

Chapter Seven ~ The Fais-Do-Do

Everyone from miles around came to the Douillard home for the evening party, with food troughs stuffed with boiled potatoes, corn, and crawfish, and Zydeco. Simple Chinese lanterns hung from the trees containing the citronella candles struggling to keep those mosquitos at bay.

The men spun yarns about Remy, his life and his escapades, knowing they could get away with quite a bit of exaggeration. God wasn't letting go of Remy to come back to correct any tales told improperly.

The women served up plates in that creole style: jambalaya, gumbo, shrimp étouffée, boudin and local brews, some straight, some flavored with honey from up the road. Life was a celebration. Death was a celebration when it came naturally. The two were connected. And somewhere in between was food.

Eugenie was serving mud pie when she noticed Roxie sitting in the corner trying to keep Pepin still. She motioned to Roxie to come to her.

"I know you're still feeling at a loss, but you know this is how we Cajuns celebrate," Eugenie said.

"I'm okay, Miss Eugenie," Roxie replied. "Just trying to get this emptiness out of my heart."

Eugenie put down her pie server and gave Roxie a tight hug. "You're young, Cher. You have many years and many people to help with that."

Paul walked up to the pie table next to his sister. "Roxie, I know this is hard. I can't make the pain go away. But maybe I can make it hurt less."

Roxie released her hug from Eugenie and wrapped her arms around her big brother. "I know, Paul. But you must be patient with me. You have to let me work into this new life I'm getting thrown into."

"Look, we have room, nice schools. You like my wife Nancy and your cousins."

"Don't expect much right off. I feel like I'm tofu in gumbo."

The three laughed as Eugenie put on a sour face thinking of tofu in a gumbo. *For shame.*

"Think of yourself as that special prize in King's Cake," said Eugenie.

"It's always about food with Cajuns. Ain't it," Paul added.

"And the parties and the Zydeco and loving life," Eugenie added.

"And the backwater and tough people living tough lives," replied Roxie.

"Now, Cher, before I go passe a slap, get out there and have some fun," urged Eugenie.

"I want to visit you every summer," Roxie said.

"Bien sur, Cher. The bayou and I welcome you any time. Paul?"

Paul replied knowing he better agree. "Don't want no cunja on me. bet you're a—"

Eugenie raised an eyebrow.

"Bet your bouille," he continued, embarrassed.

"We have plenty of that," Eugenie said. "I made some of that special. Take your sister and let's dance."

"Thanks for all you have done for her. I will keep you informed of her progress."

"We will keep in touch, young man. She has a good future ahead of her, that Roxie. I owe your father for his kindness. Take care of her for me." Eugenie began fanning herself with thoughts of her lost friend.

"Not sure I understand, but that is between the three of you. Looks like you need something to cool you down." Paul said, noticing the fanning.

Eugenie said to herself. *If you only knew.* To Paul she said, "Mais oui, mon ami. Allons."

Chapter 8 – Bobbie Lee

Bobbie Lee wet his bed again last night. Waking up in cold soaked sheets, he stared at the ceiling and sighed. The fears and humiliations had all subsided. Years of the same accidents made him as cold as his underwear.

When he awoke, he followed the same routine. Do not change. Take the sheets off the bed. Go to the backyard. Attach one side of the linens to clothesline and hold the other side off the ground with outstretched hands.

He had stopped crying, stopped looking around to see if his neighbors would see, and more importantly, stopped glancing at the kitchen window to watch his mother with folded arms and a look of disappointment.

It was never clear to him why this ritual had to take place. Would it not have been easier to put the wet clothes directly into the washer and clean them right away? Why stand out in all sorts of weather waiting for something to dry only to be put into the washer then?"

Bobbie Lee tolerated, even welcomed mornings when it rained. Not that his mother preempted the ritual, but that the sheets and his underwear would get cleaner getting soaked with fresh rain. Mother did allow for limited exposure in harsher conditions, but there was no added measure of compassion. Regardless of sun or rain, if he wet the bed, Bobbie Lee would be outside until his punishment was over.

Incontinence, as Mother called it, was a sin according to Paul's letter to Timothy. Just a verse away from "disobedient to parents", Bobbie Lee could never challenge her usage of that verse against him, even though years later he researched bed wetting. It was not totally his fault. He had a condition that made him sleep so soundly, he could not get up to go to the bathroom. His only consolation was drinking lots water at night, so his urine would not be so yellow, so strong in odor, easier to manage when standing outside in warmer weather. Urine evaporates too, along with the smell. less yellow, less discomfort.

Mother stopped trying to wake him up in the night. She thought any sort of bodily waste removal was a scourge. Yet she had the same functions as anyone else. And as Bobbie Lee learned in school, women had more discharges than men. Although she justified hers as "those blessings God has given me to bring forth life and nourish it". Unlike those references in the Bible when man is he who "pisseth against the wall."

Mother nursed Bobbie Lee when he was a baby. She used it against him many times. "I gave suck to you, gave you my own nourishment. For what? To raise a child who cannot control himself?"

Mother never admitted to him that being at her breast was so stimulating that she received strong physical pleasure from the moment. Which was why Bobbie Lee nursed until he was almost three.

Then one day she quit. There was no slow transition to milk or other liquids, no explanation, no feeling. Bobbie Lee went from Mother's milk to oatmeal, cereal, or easy-to-fix foods overnight.

Chapter Nine – Elbert and Shirley

Bobbie Lee's father was gone before he was born. Shirley Johnson met Elbert Fillmore when she was seventeen. Elbert was her first and only love. On one night of weakness, she and Elbert attempted to prove their love. Elbert lasted about five seconds, leaving her wondering. *Is that all there is?*

Of course, he blamed her for his own shortcomings, saying that she was not exciting enough, not wild enough, not anything enough. Shirley knew nothing about sex, what to do, how to do it, or what not to do. The experience left her confused, unfulfilled, and out of sheer bad timing, pregnant.

Then Elbert just left. Gone. Disappeared. Shirley was left to herself, to bear Bobbie Lee without help. Her parents labeled her a whore and offered only the "you made your bed" cliché.

Shirley left home and found a place due to the kindness of a couple down the road. They put her up above their garage. She found a menial job, enough to buy necessities for her baby. The couple who befriended her gave some assistance.

The delivery of Bobbie Lee into this world was long, painful, and lonely. The doctors and nurses were at her side, but there was little compassion for another single mother. Just the professional courtesies of the job.

Hospital stay was short, enough for the nurses to train her in breastfeeding.

Many nights followed, complicated by lack of sleep, severe and yes, warranted, depression. Bouts of crying, not from Bobbie Lee, but from herself. *How can I raise this baby on my own?* she thought.

Somewhere amidst those growing years where young children learn from their parents, when language is taught, and basic human skills are cultivated, Mother's mind went awry. It was hard to determine, the point of departure from the norm, but Mother strayed. She felt God had cursed her, labeled her with a big "W", sent her into oblivion and with a child. So, she packed up her misery and Bobbie Lee and just left.

Mother saved her meager earnings, a normal action in a trouble soul. She found a new job and a new place in Wisconsin. Mother recognized that she now needed to be in complete control, that if she were to find God's good graces again, it would be on that straight and narrow path. Mother made it so. Bobbie Lee had to follow in lock step.

Chapter Ten - Order

Maybe that was why Bobbie Lee loved Math from an early age. He saw the rigidity and unbending rules found there. 2+2 always equaled 4. Quadratic equations had only one way to be solved. There was order in numbers, order in his life. He knew where his mother stood on discipline, chores, homework, religion. Sometimes he questioned the order. He saw things in nature, despite order. There were deviations, imperfections, compromises. Yet he dared not raise those questions to Mother.

Shirley Johnson never married, never dated, never spoke of men. never spoke of Bobbie Lee's father. Bobbie Lee had seen other children enjoying times with their dads. It only took one time for Bobbie Lee to learn not to ask "Mother, where is my dad?"

After the rage and the switch and the burning backside and the deviation from the order and being sent to his room without dinner, the message was clear.

He never heard his mother cry, even after the mail came announcing the death of her parents. An Oklahoma tornado scoured the town, her childhood home, all evidence of her distant past. She stared at the letter for a little while and then it threw in the trash and cleaned the oven, even though it was not dirty.

Not long after, she was heard on the phone talking to someone. Words like inheritance, mentioning Bobbie Lee, surprise, his father. She made no emotional gestures of happiness, no tears. She hung up the phone, and noticed Bobbie Lee was watching her. Words cannot express sheer outbursts of hatred, loathing, disgust. But a mother's expression sometimes says it all.

A single phone call turned Shirley Johnson's world upside down. One minute she was the nurturer, the next minute, she became the servant.

Chapter Eleven - Inheritance

It was not until some years later that Bobbie Lee found a document in his mother's desk. It seemed that the grandparents left their inheritance to Bobbie Lee. Nothing to their daughter. The only stipulation was that she was to provide for his needs until he was eighteen. She benefited from it, but all expenses were to be accounted for. The whore was still going to be punished, but the innocent child was to be blessed.

Mother provided. Bobbie Lee was never without. She stayed at home justifying the expense as a necessity for proper nurturing and growth. She was not required to love her son according to the document. And she didn't. Dinners were provided; a comfortable home, proper clothing and education were given. Hugs? Words of encouragement? Hardly.

But Bobbie Lee got lost in his numbers. They gave him the kudos, the "*attaboys*", the job well done. The gratification was instant. Solve an equation. Make the numbers fit, and the rewards were endless. Order in all things.

He extended math into his physical world. Proper placement of clothing in drawers allowed for maximized volume management. Awakening at exactly 6 am every day. Organizing books into neat patterns on the shelves, some by height, some alphabetically, some by thickness.

Despite his almost nonexistent social skills, Bobbie Lee found math in the way his schoolmates congregated. He was always an audience never a player. He would almost predict how groups would form by gender, race, financial status, who would hook up and with whom.

Bobbie Lee loved sports. Not the playing, the excitement of winning or losing or the social aura around which sport exists. He loved the statistics, the probability, the physics behind a fly ball and the human brain being able compute when to move the legs and raise the glove to catch it. Everything came down to calculations.

Classmates frequently asked him for help in subjects in which he excelled. All of them, except PE and playground interaction. The kids stopped inviting him to play. The teachers stopped trying to buoy him up, knowing their gestures of concern were halfhearted. They knew Bobbie Lee was in his own world. And if he got some sun and fresh air and there were no altercations? Let sleeping dogs lie.

Chapter Twelve - The Playground

There was only one moment of worry. It happened only once. One of those times when a parent stands by their children in their actions. One kid, hoping to score points with the girls, and thinking Bobbie Lee was an easy target, tried pushing him around, calling him a momma's boy.

The bully pushed the wrong button. Bobbie Lee, knowing the physics behind martial arts, sent his attacker to the school hospital with a broken nose and blood all over the playground.

Mother was called to school, obviously mortified that her son had caused a problem that would have to be dealt with the bully's parents.

The principal apologized to Bobbie Lee's mother that her son was being bullied, and that a few teachers witnessed the whole thing.

"We think Bobbie Lee was just defending himself, the principal said. "The other boy has learned his lesson and will be suspended for a week."

Bobbie Lee sat quietly outside the office when his mother walked out. As usual, she said nothing. He arose out of respect, and they left the school together. The principal allowed Bobbie Lee the rest of the day off to take a breather. Nothing was said on the way home. When they arrived, Mother in a quiet voice simply said, "Go to your room, and consider your actions."

"Yes, Mother."

For the first time in her life, she had a fear in her eyes. Fear of falling off the straight and narrow. Fear of losing control. Fear of retribution. *If he did that to the bully, would he do that to me?* she thought.

After that incident, there were no more switches, no more moments of rage. She collapsed into herself and came out more determined to tighten the screws.

Instead of giving her son more room to breathe, maybe because she thought he was too confined, she went the other way. Closing in the walls around him like a trash compactor. Schedules became tighter, rules more defined, order more distinct. Bobbie Lee felt it and kept it in.

The next day at recess, everything was supposed to have been back to normal. The children played in their usual groups as Bobbie Lee was doing some measurements on shadows and solar angles, trigonometry stuff. The bully was not there, but the air in the playground was tight.

Perhaps for his personal benefit, the school did not tell the whole story. Only a few students noticed. The teachers saw it clearly. Bobbie Lee was pushed a few times before he reacted. The defensive response was quick, effective, and borderline brutal.

A rage came over the child that could have scared the bully's nose into breaking. The kid was lucky that is all that happened. The teachers saw the event as a frightening moment. One minute this disassociated child was minding his own business, the next minute could have warranted an exorcism. There was an evil in Bobbie Lee's eyes for just a moment, long enough to say to his attacker. "Next time and you're dead."

The principal debated whether to tell Mother about Bobbie Lee's reaction. They were not naive to the Johnson home life. Perhaps it was a mistake to hold back the outburst. Who would have benefited? Mother? Bobbie Lee? Who would have suffered? The incident died on the vine. Bobbie Lee never had another outburst on the playground, and he was never bullied thereafter.

Chapter 13 – The Teacher

The annual Midwest Math Camp was fast approaching, and registration was in full swing. Schools from all over the Midwest were signing up their best and brightest. Cathy Marx, Bobbie Lee's Calculus teacher, made a special trip to visit him and his mother at home to make a personal pitch, so Bobbie Lee could attend.

Some of the other teachers at the school warned Cathy about Bobbie Lee's mother. Difficult they said. Over-protective. Prone to shutting anyone down who dared make a fuss about her son's academics. Cathy was not fazed. She had worked several years with special needs children. Bobbie Lee was not a special need, but the school had to treat the mother as if he were. Besides, Cathy was simply inviting a brilliant young man to participate in a brilliant activity. Others needed to experience his prowess in math.

Bobbie Lee watched out the window as Cathy Marx came up to the house. He opened the door, greeted by a cheery yet cautious math teacher. Mother came in from the kitchen as Bobbie Lee asked the teacher to be seated. Cathy sat on the couch as Mother stood with arms folded, perturbed at the unwelcome visitor.

Cathy began. "Ms. Johnson, thank you for letting me come over. You have a lovely home."

"You are here to talk about my son and Math Camp?" Mother said coolly. There was no "thank you" or acknowledgement of the teacher.

"Yes," Cathy replied. "He is our best student, and the camp organizers have asked that he present a paper on a difficult math topic."

Mother stood still, no bristling of pride. She looked the teacher and then to her son. "And my son is the only one who can do this?" she asked.

"Well, there are many bright math students coming to this camp. We feel that Bobbie Lee is the best qualified in terms of students attending."

"What topic, may I ask, is my son addressing?"

The teacher hesitated slightly, feeling trapped, not wanting to offend Mother by assuming that she had no background in math.

"Are you familiar with the Riemann Hypothesis?" Cathy asked.

"I am not," Mother replied.

Cathy noticed a slight uneasy movement in Mother.

"But by the term hypothesis, you are implying that it is something that is just a theory?" asked Mother.

"Well, uh, yes. It is one of those mathematical ideas that does not yet have a solution," Cathy replied.

"And my son does?"

"We all wish that were the case. If he had one, he would be famous."

Mother became more agitated, thinking the whole Math Camp idea was a trap. She moved close to the chair where Bobbie Lee was seated, almost as a protective measure. But protecting him from what?

"Then why subject my son to something that has no solution?" Mother asked.

Cathy looked around the room hoping for a quick getaway from this impertinent questioning. She glanced over to a quiet Bobbie Lee hoping he would step in with some remark.

"Ms. Johnson, Bobbie Lee himself is aware of the current state of this hypothesis."

Mother stared down at her son. "Is that true?"

"Yes, Mother, but—" Bobbie Lee replied until Mother interrupted him.

"Then why are you going to talk about something that has no answer. You know how you get when you can't solve a problem."

If condescension became condensation, the whole room would have been steeped in a thick blanket of fog.

Bobbie Lee replied, "But Mother, the camp is—"

Mother again interrupted, turning her stare to the teacher. "A collection of hormone-ridden teenagers hiding behind games with numbers."

"Ms. Johnson," Cathy said, feeling perturbed. "I can assure that these are the brightest of math students in attendance. They focus on math and not much else."

"You do have social activities at these gatherings. No?" Mother asked.

"Yes, but to be honest, the activities seem to flop, because most of those attending are more interested in digits than dating."

"I see," Mother replied curtly.

Bobbie Lee grew anxious. His chances of doing something he loved and doing it away from her, was all he could think of.

"Mother, it is a chance for me to learn more things and discuss topics not covered in school," he said.

Cathy looked surprised, almost hurt, but she knew he was right. The school had its limitations. There were good students and not enough means to keep their brains involved.

"Sorry, Mrs. Marx," Bobbie Lee said. "I mean no offense. But our school can only teach so much."

"Yes, Bobbie Lee. That's correct." To Mother, Cathy said, "This is why we have these camps. Our schools just cannot feed these minds fast enough."

"And there are plenty of adults acting as chaperones at these camps?" Mother asked.

"Absolutely. Probably one adult per eight students."

"Given the math, it seems. to me to be a little sparse," Mother said.

Using math as barbs against us, Cathy thought.

"You have no need to worry about your son. Besides, he will be so busy in preparing for his topic, he won't have time for anything social."

She looked over at Bobbie Lee. "Sorry Bobbie Lee, I didn't mean—"

Bobbie Lee interrupted this time. "It's okay, Mrs. Marx. I know what you meant, and you're right."

He then turned his eyes to Mother. "Do you see any reason not to go?"

"I see a myriad of reasons not to go. But I see only one reason to go. It is what you do best," she replied.

Both Cathy and Bobbie Lee reacted in surprise. Never had such positive anything come from Mother's mouth.

Cathy, smiling, said. "You should be proud of your son, Ms. Johnson."

"Pride goes before the fall, Mrs. Marx," snapped Mother.

"I apologize. Instead, let's say your son will honor you and the math community by his attendance."

"The only honor I expect is for him to return here in one piece and not get belittled by some pranksters wanting to stir up trouble."

"Ms. Johnson, the kids who go this camp," looking at Bobbie Lee, "sorry for the stereotype," back to Mother, "are geeks and nerds. The only altercations will be who will argue what formulas are best to solve equations of four or more variables."

Mother looked confused. Yet, nothing was said directly to her that proved offensive or demeaning. Yet she still felt she was put on the defensive.

"Still, these are teenagers with nothing, but you know what on their mind," Mother said.

"Which is why we keep a close on eye on them. They are well corralled," the teacher replied trying to reassure Mother.

"You can't corral their hormones, Mrs. Marx."

"Well, um, no. But being asked to leave due to inappropriate behavior is far more a deterrent to these students than anything they can imagine. Almost like having to wear a big red 'A' on their shirt."

"Hester, Mrs. Marx, as you know, wore the red A after her adultery. Where was the self-control before the red A?"

Cathy didn't have an answer. English literature was not her forte.

Fortunately, Bobbie Lee stepped in. "Mother, you know that I am always on my best behavior."

"You had better be," Mother said.

"So, you are giving him permission to go?" Cathy asked.

Mother thought long and hard and knew that it was only a matter of time when she would no longer be able to hold him down.

"He may go, if it is that important to him."

"And to the whole math community," Bobbie Lee added.

"Thank you, Ms. Johnson," Cathy said. "You won't regret this whatsoever."

"I already have," Mother said. "My son will show you out."

Mother turned around and left the room heading back to the kitchen. There was no "goodbye", no "good luck", no "thank you for believing in my son".

Cathy looked at Bobbie Lee. She was beaming, because she felt she won. Bobbie Lee just stared as his mother left the room. There was a worried look on his face. There was no joy in the victory. No other words were needed. Cathy stood up followed by Bobbie Lee. She put her hand on his shoulder.

"You will do fine, Mr. Johnson," Cathy said. "I believe in you. We'll speak more on the subject tomorrow."

Bobbie Lee opened the door for his teacher who left with a triumphant smile. As he closed the door, he had no smile. There was just a look of dread.

This was Math Camp, he thought. *How could anything go wrong?"*

Yet sometimes in the lives of those with troubled minds, they can see into the future. Bobbie Lee was one of them.

Chapter Fourteen – Math Camp

A flurry of students began arriving, signing up for classes and being assigned to groups and teams. Each team came up with their own banners, like any other camp. Some were called the PI-rates, the Fourier Transformers, the Mobius Strippers.

Care was taken to ensure that the latter team maintained proper decorum, and the team name was allowed, although one of the team members held up a banner showing a half-naked woman dancing around the one-sided object. The banner was not approved.

One team labeled themselves the Nine Dotties, a group of nine girls who challenged everyone to solve their "think outside the box" three by three array of dots.

Most of the Dotties were from various schools in the Midwest. When they met, it was an instant connection. From day one, they were inseparable.

The mornings were spent in classes where professors from all around spouted out topics in a language only math people understood from solving complex volumes, to gaussian eliminations, to harmonic means.

Afternoons were team building exercises and down time for people to soak in what they learned. Evenings were mild social events, games and music. Not much dancing. When there was dancing, the girls would congregate in the center and dance with one another, while the boys would stand around the perimeter ogling or staring at the estrogen-powered ritual of female bonding.

Bobbie Lee's discussion on the Riemann Hypothesis went just as planned, well presented. Many came up to him to him congratulating him on a good job. Indira Patel, one of the Nine Dotties stopped him as he was walking off.

Indira was a stunning Pakistani girl. Long shimmering black hair down to her waist, perfect chocolate skin. She wore a henna tattoo on her right hand.

"You did a wonderful job," she said.

"Thank you," he replied blushing. He noticed her tattoo. It was a Sumerian symbol representing the number 31.

A Mersenne Prime, he thought. Bobbie Lee did not ask for an explanation.

"If anyone can find the solution, it would be you."

"I doubt it, but I do appreciate the confidence."

Indira noticed Bobbie Lee staring at her hand and pulled it away slowly. She wished he was like a normal boy and stared at her figure instead. She was well formed but did not flaunt her beauty. Still, she was a girl, and hoped for some male attention. But then again, she was at Math Camp.

"Perhaps if we found some time in the afternoon to talk tomorrow, I would like that," she offered.

"Talk about what?" he asked.

Indira noticing his awkward shyness, replied. "Anything that fancies you, Bobbie."

"It's Bobbie Lee."

"Okay. Bobbie Lee. If you are interested, please come see me."

"What facet of Math do you like?"

Indira was surprised at the question. Not that she couldn't answer, but that he asked. As if it were the beginning of a real conversation.

"I enjoy the mathematical order in nature, the complex ways in which patterns emerge."

"Like the Golden Ratio?"

Is there nothing he doesn't know?

"Um, yes. The patterns in how flower petals are arranged, the dimensions of the chambered nautilus."

"Hurricane spirals."

"Well, I must say, Bobbie Lee, nothing seems to escape you." Indira said impressed.

"Fibonacci Numbers, a wonderful numerical series."

To Indira, the way he spoke was almost like he was seducing her. She saw the passion in his delicious blue eyes, in his voice. It was turning her on, and suddenly, she felt uncomfortable.

"Well, I need to go," she said as a flush of warmth overtook her. "Can we continue this another time?"

"Looking forward to it, then. Tomorrow, perhaps," he said. "What is the significance of 31?"

Indira felt her skin warm even more. Not everyone would notice her tattoo, nor figure out Sumerian numbers.

"Austin and Lahore," she said as she skipped off.

Bobbie Lee knew the meaning. Both Austin, Texas and Lahore, Punjab were at latitude 31. It must have signified her current home and birthplace respectively.

He joked within himself that she would not get lost getting home or to her homeland, with a sixty-mile margin of error, of course.

Girls are weird, he thought. *Why paint themselves with something no one can read, although the artwork was impressive. Where was the longitude?* He mused and walked off.

Chapter Fifteen – The Nine Dotties

Draw a three-by-three matrix of dots. With a pencil, try to draw four straight lines through all nine dots only going through each dot once without taking the pencil off the page. It is a simple game, but it requires the person drawing to be able to solve the puzzle by going outside the array, outside the "box". There is no other way to solve it.

Nine girls met on the first day when choosing teams and decided their team name would be The Nine Dotties, daring anyone to solve them. Not only were these young women intelligent, some were blessed with extraordinary looks and figures. Any mathematician would love to study those delightful curves.

But since the boys excelled in geekiness, the Dotties were not harassed. It may have been true of the joke about how to tell a Mathematician from an Engineer: Put the Mathematicians and Engineers on the fifty-yard line and pretty girls at the goal line. Then have them go half the distance to the goal at a specified time interval. The Mathematicians would give up, knowing they would never reach the goal. Engineers, on the other hand, would win, because "it would be close enough".

The following day, for whatever reason, Bobbie Lee felt in good spirits. He had a good time learning, had strong discussions with others about various methods of solving formulas.

In the afternoon, he saw Indira with the rest of the Nine Dotties. They had separated themselves from the other teams and were going over their plans for team competitions on the following day. Indira looked quite involved with the others in the team. Yet Bobbie Lee was feeling up to talking, socializing with another student. He thought this was the best time to chat.

"Indira, hi," Bobbie Lee said.

Indira looked up, surprised and distracted. "Oh, Bobbie Lee. Um hi," she said.

"Did I get you at a bad time?" he asked.

"We were busy preparing for our competition, as you can see," Wendy Stern said. Wendy was Position 3 in the Nine Dots arrangement. She was from Illinois, a farm girl with curly blonde hair and built like she hauled a lot of hay in her summers between school. Bobbie Lee's sudden appearance annoyed her, but she was curious as to why this geek was eyeing Indira.

"It's okay, I have a few minutes," Indira said.

"Indie, we have a lot to do here," Jennifer France added. She was Velma Dinkley incarnate, the bookish wallflower from the Scooby Doo cartoon. Her forte was Mathematical Economics. She was not excited about the chances of some boy coming over and distracting her project. Jennifer was Position 4.

"Indie, who is your friend?" asked Amanda Horsch.

"This is Bobbie Lee Johnson," said Indira. "He gave the discussion on the Riemann Hypothesis."

Amanda walked up to Bobbie Lee. "Well, Mr. Johnson, nice to meet you."

Amanda Horsch, Position 1, came from Eastern Colorado. She was the tallest of the Dotties, the most voluptuous, the hottest girl at camp. Heads would turn when she walked by, and she loved every hormone-inducing act. No one ever figured out why she was even interested in math. Maybe she liked figures. She had one, and it wasn't about numbers.

"I didn't mean to interrupt," Bobbie Lee said, feeling a flush go through him just by being near Amanda.

"Riemann Hypothesis, huh? Means you're pretty smart," said Amanda.

"Well, that is why we are all here."

"Manda, you should have been there," added Indira.

"I was in the lecture on Gambling Statistics," Amanda replied. "Some card counter was sharing his experiences. He was awesome."

"Um, yeah. So much you can do with a finite set of numbers," Bobbie Lee countered.

"Well, well, Mr. Johnson, come sit right down here and share with us your wisdom."

Amanda pointed Bobbie Lee to a chair at the table where the team was working.

Indira became uneasy with Amanda's advances, knowing Bobbie Lee was in no way capable of handling Miss Position 1.

"I thought we were working on our project," Indira said.

Wendy chimed in. "Indie, if he is your friend, let the boy stay. We have time to get to know him."

"Indie, your new friend is quite the handsome gentleman," said Amanda, scooting up next to him.

"I just met him yesterday," said Indira.

"He can stay," said Annie Rhodes. "He is kind of cute, in a shy way." Annie Rhodes was Position 2, the female version of Bobbie Lee. Shy, non-descript, and a brilliant mathematician for her age. She was the go-to girl for Hyper Surface Geometry. Since she had no figure herself, she delighted in the curvature of geometrical bodies and the complex equations that accompanied them.

"I was just here to see Indira. I didn't mean to upset things," Bobbie Lee said.

"It's Indie, Bobbie Lee," said Ginger Tervil. "I'm Ginger. This is Annie, and this is Wendy," pointing to the other girls.

Ginger was everything her name implied, especially if everyone was thinking of Gilligan's Island. Enough said. Although this Ginger was not adorned in a sequin dress, she had curves that anyone interested in Hyper Surface Geometry would appreciate. Ginger was Position 7. And like the Biblical use for that number, she was complete.

"There's a dance again tonight." Amanda said. "Care to join us?" rubbing her hand along his arm and shoulder.

"I don't know," said Indira. "Maybe he is not –"

"Don't be a stick in the mud, Indie," Amanda interrupted. "Mr. Johnson here seems to enjoy the company."

Bobbie Lee was not sure what was happening inside himself. A combination of fear, excitement, frustration, embarrassment for spoiling the Dotties' plans. Whatever was happening caused an arousal in Bobbie Lee that he was making him uncomfortable.

"Mr. Johnson," Amanda said, "Tell us all about your Riemann Hypothesis for us ladies who did not make it to your lecture," rubbing his thigh.

Bobbie Lee was frozen, unable to speak. All he could hear were various voices coming from the Dotties who had surrounded him. His nose picked up a flood of scents from their bodies, their movements, their femininity. Never had these senses bombarded him before. Math never gave him those emotions. Numbers never betrayed him. He began to feel a hand where he was not expecting one to be, and in his frozen state, he was not sure what to do: Move? Resist? Succumb? Do nothing?"

The girls were laughing, not loudly to draw any attention, but more like giggling. He felt a body sit on his lap facing him. Bobbie Lee stared out into blur of hair and pastel colors.

"Manda, you don't need to do that," Indira said scolding Position 1.

"Au contraire," Amanda replied. "Mr. Bobbie Lee is enjoying this."

Amanda straddled him, slowly moving her hips across his thighs, and with any boy of teen years, the arousal was beginning to show.

"Oh my, Mr. Johnson. The other Mr. Johnson seems to be waking up."

There was more giggling from the group.

"Ooh, let's see," whispered Pei Leung, Position 6. She was the Asian pixie of the group. Tiny Pei, barely 5 feet tall. Long black hair like Indira's. And enjoying every minute of the seduction unfolding in front of her.

Amanda moved back a little for the girls to view Bobbie Lee with an erection.

"Hey, don't we think it is getting a little too much here?" Indira asked.

"Looks like your friend is liking our attention too," Pei exclaimed.

As with all senses, there is a time when it becomes too much, and the body reacts. When someone puts their hands on a hot iron, there is an immediate recoil. With a loud boom, the hands cover up the ears, or when we eat something sour or spoiled, the reaction is to spit it out. The obvious reaction happened when Amanda moved just one step too close, made one extra slide along Bobbie Lee's thigh.

His hormones reacted, and in horror with a short groan and a feeling of warm fluid in his pants he bolted up. Amanda jerked back in time to keep from being knocked down, and as he stood there with all these girls around him staring at the stain forming in his pants, all he heard was laughter. More than one source, was it two? Was it four? All nine? The Dotties were pointing at the wet spot on his pants.

Nothing his mother could do to him equaled the horror he experienced at that moment. It was the laughing and the deliberate act of being violated that caused him to run through the crowd of girls. As he ran away, others saw what happened and began laughing or snickering.

"Typical," Amanda said disgusted. "Okay, where were we?" As if nothing happened.

Chapter Sixteen – Position Six

Pei Leung, 18, was found April 1, 2010, at the northeast corner of Allied Forces Parkway and Airways Blvd, north of the Memphis International Airport. She was discovered by a couple walking south on Airways who noticed her lying among gravestones in a cemetery. She was lying on her back, arms to her side. Autopsy revealed that the victim died of asphyxiation caused by a crushed windpipe from a boot or large shoe forcibly place on her throat.

There were signs of defensive wounds, bruises on the wrists, upper arms, contusions on the back of the head. There was no sexual contact. The victim was still a virgin. However, a pool of semen was found in her navel, placed there postmortem. DNA from the semen did not match any known records in local or federal databases. There were no drugs in her system. Stomach contents revealed a small amount of fruit juice. Time of death was between midnight and one am.

Miss Leung was a student in Physics at University of Memphis. Her parents recently moved to Russellville, Arkansas, where her father Eddie Leung was a Nuclear Physicist at the Arkansas Nuclear One Reactor. According to her parents and friends, Miss Leung was not involved in any relationships.

Due to the suspicious nature of the semen deposit, the FBI was brought in on the case. Agent Roxanne

Cormier was called in as liaison between the FBI and local law enforcement. She worked out of the New Orleans office and was asked to participate in the case as part of a research project profiling sexually-based crimes. Memphis PD Lieutenant Graham was primary lead for the case.

"Agent Cormier," said Graham. "We're glad to have you as a part of the team. We called you here due to the strange nature behind the discovery of Miss Leung."

"It's a pleasure, Sir," said Roxie. "Our research project, once complete, will benefit agencies both local and federal when it comes to case as we have here."

"Have you seen a situation like this before?"

"No, Sir. We know from what evidence that has been obtained that this is not a sex crime."

"Because there was no sexual contact? What about the pool of semen in her navel?"

"The absence of penetration in any cavity: oral, anal, or vaginal or less common places such as axillary—"

Graham interrupted. "Axillary?"

"Armpit, Sir. This implies the perpetrator was sending a message."

"The victim did not have any boyfriends that we are aware of."

"The killer was not impotent, due to the pool of semen itself. There was a high sperm count and it was neatly placed in the navel suggesting the killer had staged the body, removed her clothes and then ejaculated."

"Sounds like he was sending a message. Any idea as to what?"

"That is anyone's guess. I would say he was doing it to embarrass her. Retribution perhaps?"

"Does this cross reference with any other cases?"

"Not a specific one like this. Other instances where a person had a pulled out during a rape, so he wouldn't get his victim pregnant."

"How thoughtful."

"Yes. Or he masturbated before he penetrated his victim. But this one was calculated and executed with precision because there was no semen elsewhere on the body."

"So, we are looking at a revenge killing with a hygiene component?"

"We cannot rule out something other than revenge, but the meticulous manner of pooling the semen does create a new profile. Are there any leads?"

"None right now. No DNA match, no fingerprints. A few fibers. The lab is checking on those. No blood besides the victim's. No skin cells under the fingernails."

"Cameras?"

"There is a learning academy just north of where the body was found. None was pointing toward the cemetery. The killer may have entered through the groves of trees to the east of the cemetery, dropped the body and went back the way he came in, unseen."

"Any reason to suppose that Miss Leung was deliberately there on the street corner?"

"According to friends and family, she was a model student, extremely intelligent, good natured. She lived near the university and had no reason to be in that part of town after midnight. She didn't drink, so there was probably no bar involved."

"So, she was bought there by someone she may have known?"

"A fellow student perhaps. We don't know. Our focus now is more canvassing the school and the area where she lived. She didn't work, so there was no job component."

"Says here stomach contents was fruit juice. Any lead on that."

"No. The lab says it was generic. Could have come from any source."

"So, we are at a dead end until we get some new information."

"Sadly, yes."

"And then there is the issue with the body being arranged deliberately," Roxie said.

Graham replied, "Yeah, quite neatly, almost at attention.

"Is the cemetery still secure?"

"It is. Do you want to see the place for yourself? Our crime scene investigators have been all over the place."

"Fresh set of eyes."

"Of course. Officer Putney and I will take you there."

"Officer Graham. I'm only here to collect information to build a profile, not to scrutinize your work."

"I know, Agent Cormier."

Chapter Seventeen – The Cemetery

The cemetery was situated at the intersection of Allied and Airways. It was a small plot of land about 1 acre. There was a line of trees to the east, the parkway to the west, the learning academy on the north, and a parking lot on the south. Cormier and the other policemen arrived and went toward the only gate on the south side.

"Agent Cormier, this is the location where the body placed."

"When you say placed, you are assuming that he deliberately positioned her?"

"All I know is she was lying like so, hands to her side."

"I wonder why she was placed so close to the road. Would it not have been easier to dump her in the woods back there?"

"Yes. I wondered that myself."

"For someone to find her more easily?"

"Perhaps."

"You think there is a cemetery connection?"

"The girl was Chinese. This is a Jewish cemetery. We should speak to the rabbi of the congregation. Pass her photo around just to make sure."

"Good idea. Isn't there something in the Bible about spilling your seed?"

"Not well versed on the scriptures, Agent Cormier, but if it clicks in your head, I will have someone consider it. Maybe ask the rabbi."

"I was not expecting a religious component, but it adds nicely to the weird profile we are creating. Guy takes girl. She struggles. He takes her to a cemetery, crushes her windpipe hard enough the break her neck, and then ejaculates on her."

A small building sat south of the cemetery. Perhaps it was a place of worship or just for pre-burial services. A single car was parked in the lot, amid the other police vans and equipment.

An old man stood at the door of the building with his hands clasped behind him. He was wearing a black vest, black trousers, which contrasted with his long white beard and the obvious payot, or curls, which hung down in front of his ears. He dressed as a Hasidic Jew. Probably the rabbi of the congregation.

Roxie and Graham noticed him staring at them, with a look of displeasure. And for good reason. His surroundings were desecrated. As they approached, the man in the door straightened up and walked toward them as they held out their badges.

Graham reached out his hand. "Excuse me. Rabbi?"

The man took Graham's hand. "Yes. I am Rabbi Kohen. Is this about the woman you found?"

Roxie extended her hand. The rabbi quickly returned his hands behind his back and slightly bowed. Roxie got the message.

"Apologies, Rabbi." Roxie said. "Yes, this is about the woman found in the cemetery."

"How may I help you?" Kohen asked.

"Please forgive us for intruding," said Graham, showing the rabbi a picture of Pei Leung, "Have you seen her before."

"Such a young thing. Such a shame, May God give her peace. No, I have not seen her. She looks Asian. Correct?"

"Yes, Rabbi. I imagine she was not associated with your congregation."

"I am sorry to say that we do not have any Asians in our congregation. We also do not have any young men that I know of, dating an Asian girl."

"Good to know. Then we won't have to bother the members of your congregation, but we could leave a picture, just in case," Roxie said, giving some comfort to the rabbi on behalf of his members.

"Of course, of course," the rabbi said nodding and frowning.

Graham then asked. "One more question. Isn't there a reference in the scriptures, about 'spilling one's seed'?"

"Oh my, yes. Was this girl raped?" the rabbi asked with a show of sadness and surprise.

"No, she wasn't. But there was semen found on her."

"There was a man named Onan who was told by God to have children with a woman named Tamar." Kohen said. "He refused, knowing that any child he was to bear would not become his heir. So, he spilled his seed on the ground. I don't think that needs further explanation."

"No, Rabbi. It's quite clear."

"God was displeased with Onan and he slew him for disobedience."

"A harsh punishment. I can't imagine God doing that today."

"We disobey God. We leave it up to him to determine the consequences."

"Thank you for your time."

"I will call you, if someone recognizes the girl. Please pass my condolences on to the parents."

"Of course, Rabbi."

The agents left the rabbi and returned to the car.

Roxie said, "Spilling seed? Disobedience? Punishment from God? I doubt we have a religious factor to this case."

"What make you think that?"

"The crushed windpipe. That and the semen must be connected."

"Could not have been rough sex because she was still a virgin."

"The coroner said there were defensive wounds. She tried to fight her attacker, but he got the upper hand, got her down on the ground in such a manner to put his shoe or boot to her throat. That was the final strike."

"And the semen is his calling card?"

"He was trying to say something."

Chapter Eighteen – Position Three

Wendy Stern, age 20. Married to Jared Stern. Lived in Springfield, IL. They were newlyweds. No children. She was a tutor at various elementary schools in the area. Her body was found on January 24, 2013, at the intersection of Mason and County Road 2800 North, near Armington, Illinois, approximately fifty-four miles from her home. The victim was lying face up in the center of the intersection, fully clothed, with her hands at her side.

Livor mortis revealed that she died at the scene and was not moved. The autopsy determined the cause of death was asphyxiation due to a crushed windpipe with enough force to break her neck at C5-C6 vertebrae.

In addition, there was considerable bruising on her body, suggesting defensive wounds. Ligature marks at her wrists indicate she was tied up. The coroner at the scene found a pool of semen in her navel. Evidence shows it was placed there postmortem since it looked undisturbed.

Ambient and core body temperatures place her death between 11:30 pm and 1:30 am.

Skin cells found underneath her fingers matched the DNA of the semen. There were no hits on any DNA databases. A small piece of plastic was discovered lodged between teeth 7 and 8. Lab results determined that the plastic was like a painter's tarp, available at any hardware store. A rape kit determined there was no sign of sexual contact.

Her husband had reported her missing at ten pm the night of the 23rd. She was last seen at the school where she was tutoring approximately 5:30 pm. The victim's husband was not ruled a suspect. He was working until seven pm, went home directly from work. Phone records show that he had been calling friends to find his wife until midnight. He then drove to her parent's house five minutes away and was there the rest of the night. A farmer found her around seven am driving his tractor to an adjacent field.

Investigators questioning the victim's husband revealed no known enemies. She was well-liked by neighbors, faculty, and students. The area where the body was discovered is sparsely populated. The investigators met with the homeowners south and east of the inter-section. Nothing suspicious was reported. The case files were sent to Pekin County Sheriff's Office.

Chapter Nineteen – The Stairs

Bobbie Lee walked in the front door after school and was met with dead silence. Not the usual TV being on or the stereo playing. Just funeral home quiet. He did not bother announcing his perfunctory "Mother, I'm home."

He quietly walked through the kitchen and noticed that the basement door was open. He went to the top of the stairs and saw his mother lying still at the bottom.

Apparently, she tripped and fell carrying a box of items to the basement. The box and its contents were strewn on the floor around her. Bobbie Lee went to the phone.

"911. What is your emergency?"

"I came home from school and found my mother lying at the bottom of the stairs," he explained.

"Is she breathing?"

"No, looks like she has been here a while. There is dried blood on her head, and she is not moving."

"Alright. Stay calm. We will send someone out right away."

Bobbie hung up the phone and walked down the stairs to the basement. As he rearranged her position, he looked down at his mother.

"You called me incontinent. You called me a horny teenager. I did the math a long time ago. You were the horny teenager, and oh yes, you got pregnant. You did the dirty deed, Mother, and you throw out all your pious preaching and condemnations for impurity. Now, look where you are. You're lying in your own dead filth."

The emergency response was quicker than expected. Bobbie Lee rushed to the front door and paramedics hurried through as he pointed the way to the basement door. Behind the paramedics entered officer Williams.

"Are you the one who called?" asked Williams.

Bobbie responded, "Yes, Sir."

"Shall we go see what happened?"

"If you don't mind Sir. I will wait in here. We can talk after you see my mother." He spoke as if through the actor's mask of a distressed child.

"As you wish. Stay right here."

Williams was gone for a few minutes. Bobbie heard the officer talking with the paramedics. It sounded like there was movement on the stairs, trying to get his mother out of the basement. The officer returned to the living room. Bobbie Lee just stared off into nowhere.

"You okay, son?"

"Is my mother alright?"

"I'm afraid not. She had been lying there for a long time. I can't say for certain, but the fall may have broken her neck."

Bobbie asked, desiring to know, "Did she suffer?" He hoped that she lay there alive feeling every bit of pain a human could take.

Williams replied, lying, "I don't think so, but medical examiner will have to decide."

Bobbie looked down at his lap, rejoicing inside but never showing his relief, only a fake sadness.

"May I ask you a few questions?"

"Yes, of course."

"You arrived home at what time?"

"3:14."

"3:14." Williams said, surprised. "Quite exact."

"It is the usual time I get home. Plus, 3:14 is a number I remember: PI. You know 3.14."

"Um, sure. Okay, did anything seem odd when you walked in?"

"Yes, it was quiet. Mother didn't like quiet. Something was always on: radio, TV, stereo. but it was quiet."

"Did you call out to her?"

"Yes, Sir. I told her I was home. She expects that."

Williams noted the use of the present tense.

"I see. Okay. When you did not get a reply, what did you do?"

"First instinct was to go the kitchen."

"Why is that?"

"I thought she would be there at the table, reading or cleaning."

"That was when you noticed the basement door open."

"Yes, Sir. That was when I looked and saw Mother at the bottom."

"Did you go down to help her, and see if she was still alive?"

"No, Sir. I knew that if I called 911, someone would come, and I didn't want to disturb the conditions in which Mother lay."

"Well, that makes sense, Mr. Johnson. Were you at school all day? You didn't come home for lunch?"

"No, Sir. I had been at school since seven, working on some projects."

"When was the last time you saw or spoke to your mother?"

"Before I left. She said she was going to do some work cleaning out the garden before winter."

"Is that why she still had her garden boots and work clothes on when you saw her?"

"Yes, Sir. I guess so."

"Any arguments before you left? Anything she said to you?"

"No, Sir. The only thing she said was to remind me that I had work to do in the garage after school."

"And that was normal for you to be given chores like that? Nothing out of the ordinary?"

"That was the normal thing after school, yes."

"You keep a tidy house here. Everything appears. to be in their proper order."

"Yes. That is Mother's wish."

"And when you came in, nothing was out of place?"

"The only thing out of place was the open door to the basement. It is never open unless someone goes down there. That is why I came to the doorway, because it was different."

"And you saw your mother at the bottom of the stairs and called 911."

"Yes."

"Immediately?"

"It took a moment for me to process what I saw. It could not have been more than a minute or two."

"Did you and your mother have a good relationship?"

"As good as anyone can have. Single mother raising a child."

"Where is your father?"

"I do not know. I never knew him. Mother never discussed him. He was never a topic to bring up to her."

"I see. Would you ever hurt your mother?"

"No, Sir. She was all I had," he lied. What a poor innocent victim: the epitome of the Yiddish word chutzpah, where a son would kill his own parents, so he could be labeled an orphan.

"Mr. Johnson—"

"Bobbie Lee, please."

"Okay, Bobbie Lee. I think that's enough for now. If I have more questions, I will come back."

"Or call."

"What will you do now?"

"I am an adult, sir. I can take care of myself. The house is paid for. My grandparents left me some money. I will be okay."

"Right. When we have finished with your mother, you will be notified to make the proper arrangements."

"Thank you, Officer Williams."

Williams and the Crime Scene Team left with all their equipment, and especially, with the body of Shirley Johnson. Bobbie Lee felt the silence descend upon him like a warm blanket, followed by a slight tingle of relief. No more demeaning comments, no more stares of disappointments.

He walked up to his bedroom and turned on B.B King and listened to "Free". His soul was filled with a strange desire. *I love you babe*, he thought.

Chapter Twenty – The Coroner's Office

The following day, Office Williams went to the Medical Examiner's office in Oneida County in Rhinelander, Wisconsin. Forest County contracts with them. Doctor Schiff was the ME on call. Williams found him in one of the autopsy rooms.

"Can you tell me anything about the victim?" asked Williams.

"Looks like a typical fall," Schiff replied. "She was carrying a box of items. She probably missed a step with her garden boots and fell."

"Time of death?"

"Noon to 1 pm. Death was not immediate. There were dried tears. No sign of trying to move."

"Any sign of being helped down the stairs? Any defensive wounds?"

"No. It looked like a clean fall. Bruises caused by hitting the steps and railing. I didn't see any sign of foul play."

"No other clues? Anything in her clothes suggesting something suspicious?"

"Her boots may have been the cause. Worn soles. Not enough tread. Perhaps she didn't see the next step because of the box she was carrying. There was slight osteoporosis, but she was young only in her late 30's. A healthy attractive woman, still able to have children. No signs of any sexual contact. Breasts indicative of a woman who nursed a lot."

"A lot?"

"Seems like she could have nursed her son longer than normal, maybe into his second or third year."

"Sounds a little creepy."

"Not at all. There are instances of women nursing up to age five. There are also cases of ANR, Adult Nurturing Relationship, where women lactate in their 40s or later, because they nurse adult men."

"That's sick. You think this was the case with her son?"

"Oh no. She had not lactated for many years."

"So, you're calling this an accidental death."

"Have to. I see no further evidence. Why? Do you think her son had a hand in it?"

"Well, I don't see an Oedipus Complex here, but when I talked to him, he was empty."

"Could be shock."

"Well, with shock, there is an emotion of some degree. This guy had nothing. More like 'Hi Mom. I'm home.

Oh, you're dead. Should've been more careful. Bummer. Guess I will have to make my own dinner.'"

"I'm sorry, detective. I can only rule on an accidental death. But her tox screens have not come back to see if she had been drinking or taking drugs."

"Alright. Let me know if anything comes back suspicious."

"Will do. In the meantime, if the son asks about when he can have his mother's body, tell him my office will call him."

"I have a feeling he won't be sitting by the phone."

A few days later, the Medical Examiner's office called the Johnson home. There was no answer. They left a voicemail.

Chapter 21 – Position Two

Annie Rhodes, age 25, was murdered on November 11, 2015. Her body was found at the intersection of 150th Street and Vanilla, 9 miles west of Creston Iowa. She lived in Leawood, Kansas, approximately 170 miles from the scene of the crime.

The victim was clothed but not wearing a coat, lying face up. Her body had been positioned with her arms at her side. Death was caused by blunt force trauma to the throat, crushing her windpipe resulting in asphyxiation. Defensive bruises were found on her arms and legs. She also suffered a contusion to the left side of the head. Police at the scene reported a translucent liquid in the corner of her right eye. Autopsy confirmed that the liquid was semen. DNA analysis revealed no matches in local databases. The medical examiner placed the time of death around two am.

The report also showed that she was tied at her wrists and ankles. Fibers found in the victim's hair were similar to carpet fibers found in automobiles. Lab results have yet to pinpoint make and model. There was no residue under her fingernails. The autopsy also determined there was no sexual contact. The victim was wearing a tampon. Bruising on the inner thighs may have been caused by the attacker during a struggle.

Miss Rhodes was not married but she had a child age five. The family reported that she was seeing someone at the time of her death, a Mr. Joseph Lynch. He was on an assignment for his company in Phoenix at the time of the murder. When the victim did not return home, the babysitter had tried many times to contact her by phone. At 10:45, she called Leawood police reporting her missing. She was last seen leaving her home at seven pm. The babysitter said she was going out to meet an old friend.

Miss Rhodes' body was found by a homeowner living just south of said intersection. Other homes in the area were canvassed. No one saw or heard anything out of the ordinary.

Union County Sheriff's office forwarded the case files to Des Moines Police Department for a more thorough review.

Chapter Twenty-Two – Position Four

Jennifer France, age 26, married to Willie France, was murdered July 14, 2016. The Frances lived in Pueblo, Colorado. They had one child. The body of Mrs. France was located approximately 360 miles away near Beaver, Oklahoma. She was found at the center of the intersection of EW-32 and NS-143 23 miles south of Beaver. The victim was clothed, lying face up with hands positioned at her side. Cause of death: crushed windpipe leading to asphyxiation. Livor mortis showed that she died at the scene. There was no evidence of sexual contact, however the victim may have engaged in sexual activity within the past 36 hours. A small amount of semen was found in the vaginal canal.

Another collection of semen was found on her lips, placed there postmortem. The mouth was almost fully closed, and the semen seeped between the lips, some had run down the side of her face. DNA revealed that the semen in the vaginal canal was that of the husband. The other semen belonged to another person. No matches were found in the system.

Carpet fibers were found in her hair and on her clothing. Lab results on the fibers were inconclusive. Time of death was between the hours of midnight and 3 am. There were no bruises suggesting a struggle. Tox screens reported elevated amounts of Temazepam which may have been used as a knockout drug. This was consistent with the long distance she traveled before she was killed.

A woman who was heading to a church east of the intersection, found the body approximately 6:30 am.

Mrs. France was last seen leaving her job at 5:30. She was an engineer at a local firm in Pueblo. Phone records showed she called her husband at home at 5:33. She stated that she was meeting an old friend on the way home. She never arrived. Her husband began calling all her known friends. No one made any appointment to see her. At 11:15, her husband called Pueblo Police and reported her missing. Her vehicle was later found at a Hampton Inn off I-25 south of Pueblo. The hotel cameras did not provide any extra information. No one at the hotel saw Mrs. France when shown her photo.

Authorities of Beaver County, Oklahoma turned over the case files to Pueblo Police Department.

Chapter Twenty-Three ~ Position Seven

Two employees of Slater Natural Resources were driving to work from their homes in Barnhart, Texas, when they discovered a body on Highway 163 about a mile south of their workplace. The victim was identified as Ginger Tervil from Dallas, Texas. She was found at 5:30 am on March 29, 2017.

Miss Tervil was reported missing the night before, by her father, Jack Tervil. She was twenty-five. She worked as an actuary for a company in Arlington. The employees who found the body immediately called 911. Approximately seven minutes later, the Barnhart Fire Department arrived. They had called for assistance from Ozona, Texas, about forty miles away. An RN from Slater also came down to offer assistance, having heard it on her scanner.

The victim was lying on her back, hands at her side. She was wearing only a skirt and panties. The medical examiner of Crockett County who was assigned to the case, had determined that Miss Tervil was killed by a forcible blow to her throat. Marks around her neck suggested her throat was crushed by a boot or heavy shoe. Livor mortis indicated she died at the scene.

Miss Tervil did not suffer any sexual attack, however the exposed portion of her chest showed amounts of semen on her breasts. Her wrists, ankles, and axillary regions revealed she was tied with a rope so tight, there was blood loss in the right arm. Bruising patterns on arms, feet, thighs and back showed a significant attempt to free herself and some parts of her hands displayed defensive marks.

Blood and skin under her nails showed she may have scratched her attacker. The blood matched the DNA in the semen. Rigor mortis was setting in when she was discovered. Time of death was just after midnight.

Officials from Irion County spoke to locals in the small towns of Barnhart, Mertzon, and Sherwood. Reagan County was asked to get involved. Sheriffs asked around the truck stop in Big Lake, if they had seen or heard any disturbance.

A cashier behind the register noticed a young man middle 20's with a cut on the side of his neck. The woman asked if he was okay. She said he was polite and yes, he was okay. He said his dog needed a nature break and scratched him from behind. The cashier did not give it another thought. She had dogs that did the same thing. He purchased a 44-ounce drink and some Neosporin. It was late at night, and he disappeared down the road.

The case files were handed over to San Angelo Police Department, since it was the largest facility in the area.

Chapter Twenty-Four ~ Moyes

FBI Agent Lester Michaels, from the St. Louis, Missouri office, was given the assignment to find Roxie Cormier and bring her back to his office. He had spent many years with the ABC Organizations in various offices throughout the lower forty-eight. He had only been in the Midwest Regional area for a short time and had not acclimated to the heavy Louisiana air as he drove into bayou country.

It was not lost on anyone as Michaels walked into Moyes Swamp Tours, that his attire was not appropriate to his task at hand. Long sleeve button down shirt, khakis, expensive leather shoes.

Behind the counter sat a large black man, more like a mountain with legs.

Probably played tackle for LSU, Michaels thought.

As he approached the counter, the mountain, not distracted by the visitor kept his eyes on whatever he was doing and asked, "Help you?"

"You Moyes?" Les asked.

"I could be," replied the mountain.

"Your web site has a photo of you with your name under it."

"Maybe it's my little brother. You booking a tour?"

"I'm looking for someone."

The man looked up at Les and gave an annoyed stare.

"Man, this ain't no information kiosk in the mall."

Les flashed his badge. "Lester Michaels, FBI, Midwest Region."

"My cousin got one of them out da cereal box featuring G-Men," Moyes replied.

Les returned his badge to his pocket. "Roxanne Cormier dit Boucher. You know her?"

"Lotta French you just spit out there. I look like a translator to you?"

"You know Roxanne? I hear she hangs out down here around this time of year."

"Miss Cormier in the backwater somewhere. Why you need her?"

"High School reunion."

"Not your class, Mr. G Man."

"Look, Moyes I—"

"Mr. Moyes to you. I run a respectable business here. I got folks coming from all over the world want to see the swamp. Not here to have face time with no white boy from up north."

"Please accept my apology, Mr. Moyes."

"Now, what you want with Roxie?"

"She is FBI. We need her. I hear she is a tracker."

"A cracker tracker," said Moyes laughing. "She the best in these parts. Ain't no one slip away from her and not look over they shoulder the rest of they lives."

"Where can I find her?"

"You ain't gonna find her without GPS. You got one of those?"

"Yeah, state of the art. Find your location within a meter."

"You gonna need a meter out here, boy. Out here, one meter can mean you get back in one piece, or you swamp food."

"You know how I can get to her?"

"Only one way far as you're concerned."

"I'm listening."

"Get your cracker ass in your car and drive that rental back up 307 where you came from."

"I'm not leaving until I get Rox—" Les broke out his wallet and dropped fifty on the counter.

"Man, don't go trying to bribe my ass," Moyes interrupted. "Your dead presidents ain't worth jack, unless you're itching for a tour. My boy Jesse here, we do fine. We have a great business running people down the bayous, scaring white folk and Asians."

Moyes changed his accent from deep south to a refined northern one.

"My colleague Jesse Franks and I are from Cleveland. We both have degrees in Marketing. We came down here and bought this swamp tour business. It is a thriving venture. And you coming down here does not look good for the tourists. Now do you want my help?"

"Look, I'm sorry. I am in a rush. I need Ms. Cormier dit Boucher."

Moyes returned to his deep accent. "Get your ass back up 307 to the Honey Store. Buy three jars of local honey. Come back here. You bring the honey. You get the coordinates."

"Why honey?"

Moyes didn't need to reply. He just stood up and placed his monster hands on the counter and motioned with his head the direction of the door.

"Alright, if you say so."

As he was leaving, Les heard behind him *cracker ass*, and then laughing.

Thirty minutes and three jars of golden treasure later, Michaels walked back into Moyes' office. He set the jars on the counter. Moyes handed him a piece of paper, slid two jars toward Les and moved the third to a shelf below the counter.

"You take this honey to these coordinates. You ask for Miss Douillard. She knows where Roxie is. The honey is a gift. Your Ulysses Grants won't be worth anything where you're going."

"What about that third jar?"

"Every man has his price, Mr. G Man. Every man has his price."

"What road do I take?"

Raucous laughing was heard from Moyes and Jesse, who was sitting at a table preparing tickets for the first tour of the day.

"Man, ain't no roads where you going. Unless you take a pirogue."

Moyes pointed to an old black man reading the paper in the corner of the waiting area. "My esteemed associate Mr. Reginald Boudin there would gladly loan one of his fine craft for your traveling pleasure. You flash one of your fifties to him, he would be much obliged."

Boudin spoke up. "Another one of those fifties and I might even put in enough gas for you to get back."

More laughing.

Moyes added, "All about business, Mr. FBI."

"This feels like Sherwood Forest," Les said.

Moyes in a well-spoken British accent replied, "And I am Robin Hood sans tights."

Laughing.

"Cheers Mr. Michaels. Kindly return Mr. Boudin's boat better than you collected it."

There wasn't much else to say. Old Boudin creaked up out of his chair and motioned for the agent to follow him out the back and down to the docks where all the boats were moored. Boudin pointed to one of the pirogues tied up. He held out his hand awaiting payment.

"You know how to run an outboard, Agent Michaels?" asked Boudin.

Les looked over the neatly cared for vessel and its outboard.

"Pull out the choke, pull the cord, untie the lines, put her in gear," replied Les.

"They teach you well at the academy, Sir. Keep to the right. Don't be getting too near the trees along the shore. Ya hear?"

"Don't want to run her aground?" Les asked.

Boudin just laughed and shook his head. "No, Sir. Were it dat easy. Snakes. You don't need no moccasin crawling in and riding up the bayou with you."

The sweat forming around Les' forehead was not caused by the humidity. He didn't mind snakes. Just didn't want one to surprise him.

"Thanks for the advice, Mr. Boudin."

"Pleasure's mine. Anything to help the FBI, and Miss Cormier, of course."

Les stepped into the pirogue, and got the motor started on the first pull. When Boudin felt reassured his craft was safe, he untied the lines, and Les slowly pulled away from the dock.

"When you see Miss Douillard, please tell her I said hello. And mind your manners around those ladies: her and Miss Cormier. This may be the backwater, but they proper and deserve right."

Less slightly bowed his head and replied, "Yes, Sir. I shall."

Boudin watched as Les motored away, and then strolled back in the office.

"He okay?" Moyes asked, seeing a worried look on Boudin's face.

"Someone asking to fetch Miss Roxie, mean something bad," replied Boudin.

"Damn right. Somebody in a world of hurt if Roxie gets called. He pay you for your services?"

Boudin pulled out two crisp fifties and laughed. "Our taxpayer dollars at work."

"Cracker." Moyes replied, then whispered to himself as he went back to whatever he was doing, "Yep, someone in a big hurt, and they getting the *cunja*."

Chapter Twenty-Five – Fanning

Les steered the rental boat down Douillard channel. A dog different than many years prior, announced the arrival of the stranger. As Les approached, Eugenie Douillard appeared out of the trees and walked toward the dock.

"Rudy, sit," she said to the dog. Rudy stopped barking and sat still watching the arrival of the visitor.

"Help you? You lost?" Eugenie asked.

"Ms. Douillard?"

"Yes. I wasn't expecting any visitors."

"I am looking for a Roxanne Cormier dit Boucher."

"Not here."

Agent Michaels took out the honey jars and set them gently on the dock. Eugenie eyes grew large upon seeing the stranger's gift.

"If only I were thirty years younger, Sir. Who might you be, bringing gifts of gold to an old woman?"

Les showed his badge. "Lester Michaels, FBI. It's important that I find Roxanne. I heard she was here."

"Folks in town tell you that?"

"Yes. A Mr. Moyes. He gave me directions here."

"Well, he was kind enough to tell you my weakness. Come on in and set a spell."

Les grabbed the honey, placed the jars in a small knapsack and followed Eugenie into the house with Rudy close behind.

"Put the jars over there by the fridge, Mr. Michaels," Eugenie said, pointing to the counter. "Now, what on earth does a city boy like you want with Miss Roxie?"

"Why do people keep calling me a city boy?"

"Cher, makes no never mind." Eugenie replied, eying Michaels' not-for-the-bayou outfit. "You say you're FBI? Then you know why Roxie is down here."

"All I know is she is supposed to be here; the office needs her. I have come to bring her back. I understand she is a tracker."

Eugenie "Best dang tracker south of the arctic circle. Hmm. FBI. Tracker. Roxie. Someone lost? Someone run away?"

"She is also a profiler. Looks like we have a case matching one of hers that went cold from a few years back."

"Oh my. She is out on the bayou somewhere, prepping for a week-long camp for troubled children. They come from all over: Jackson, New Orleans, Baton Rouge, Gulfport. She gives them a taste of an unforgiving environment that makes their pitiful lives seem like Disneyland. Most leave with a better attitude, some leave scared. Everyone leaves vowing not to come back."

"I guess she knows these parts well?"

"She knows every inch of this place, ever since she was a child. She and her father explored every bayou in this area. No one can hide without Roxie sniffing them out."

"How do I find her?"

"She ain't here. But give it a little time. She'll show up."

"When? Ten minutes? Ten hours?"

Eugenie looked the agent up and down, shaking her head. "Mr. Michaels, you are a city boy. All rush, rush, and such. We don't hurry down here. Life is slow, like the back water. When you settle down to the flow of the bayou, she will appear."

"Well, Miss Douillard, then you will have to keep me company."

Eugenie started fanning herself, the air began to get warm around her.

"If only I were thirty years younger, Mr. Michaels."

"Les, please."

"Mr. Michaels works for me. I am a proper Southern lady. I may not be fighting to get into playing the back nine at Augusta or having tea with the New Orleans cotillions, but I know my manners even in the backwoods here."

Les embarrassed, said, "Suit yourself, Miss Douillard."

"Eugenie, please."

"Tit for tat, Miss Douillard."

"Suit yourself. So, what do you know about Roxie?"

"All I know of her is her background in the FBI. Bachelor's degree from LSU in Anthropology. Master's in Psychology from Northwestern. Emphasis on Criminal Behavior. Came to work for the FBI after school, made a name for herself after a year or two after finding people that others couldn't. Seems she has a sense about people, eidetic memory, never married, lived with her brother and his wife before college. Before then, I guess she lived down here somewhere with her father, a man named Remy Cormier dit Rocher."

Upon hearing Remy's name, Les noticed Eugenie sitting back in her chair taking a deep breath, fanning herself some more.

"Yes Remy, a gentleman of gentlemen. Brought me honey," Eugenie said in a pensive tone.

"I guess you knew him well. With all the added fanning?"

"Well, Mr. Michaels, a lady does not share intimate moments with a stranger."

"You two were an item?"

"For shame. No, Mr. Michaels. Ain't no tabloid fodder history gossip come out of my relationship with Monsieur Remy. We were friends."

"I am sorry. You just seemed to perk up a little when I mentioned his name."

"You FBI people, you don't miss a beat, now do you? Yes, I had feelings for him. I am a widow, so was he. He always came by for friendly visits, bringing me honey, bringing Roxie. Such a delightful child. Smart, lovely. Loved her father. He did a favor for me one time that I was never able to return."

"May I ask what he did for you? Promise it won't leave the bayou."

"Sir, nothing leaves here that ain't meant to leave."

"Meaning?"

"One day some men came down the backwater from Vacherie, a little spot on Lac des Allemands. Hunters or fishermen, looking for a prize to take home. You know boating and drinking don't mix, whether you are on the gulf or in a bayou, Mr. Michaels. These men saw me on my dock fishing, minding my business. They came up making a noise and disrupting the quiet of this place."

"That is one thing about this place." Les said. "Lots of quiet. I take it that they did not act gentlemanly."

"No, Sir. They did not. If it weren't for Remy just happening to drop by, I am not sure what they would have done. I don't even want to imagine. Remy scared them off. Didn't need a 'local' getting in the way of their drunken fun. Bad thing though. They said they would be back."

"Did they come back?"

"Remy. Bless his heart. Said he would make sure that did not happen. Funny thing, Mr. Michaels, they never came back. Either they got sober, got lost or whatever, I did not pay it any mind."

"And Remy? Did he take care of it?"

"Well, Mr. Michaels, I cannot say. All I know for sure is a few days later, I heard Remy's outboard sputtering up to my dock. I went out to meet him. He spoke kindly to me like he always does, handed me a few jars of honey, and said with a wry grin. 'Your honey is safe'. Well, he tipped his hat, and said nothing more. Turned his pirogue around and motored off. Sometimes in my quiet moments, I always wondered if in his comment, there was a double entendre, but you know, as a lady, I had to dismiss such a thought. Mercy me." Eugenie said, fanning herself even more.

"That was it?"

"That was all. Didn't want to know any more. Didn't ask. I yelled at him as he was heading down the channel, I owe you Mr. Cormier dit Boucher."

"Did you ever return his favor?"

"Wasn't much chance. Next week he and Roxie came up to visit Bayou Piquant. Something happened in the backwater. Moccasin got him. Roxie couldn't get him back in time. The man passed on leaving us all to grieve a terrible loss."

"I am so sorry. You had feelings for him, didn't you?"

"Yes, sir. To be honest, I did. Real gentlemen hard to find out here. He made me feel safe. Last words from him was 'I like you, Miss Eugenie'. Seemed contrived to me, but I held on to that thought all these years."

"What happened to Roxie after his death? Did she come live with you?"

"Mercy no. A child like that needed a life outside the bayou, proper schooling, something more refined than me."

"Well, I have only known you a short while, Miss Douillard. You're a true lady. She would have grown to be like you in all your proper ways."

"My, my, Mr. Michaels, if only I were thirty years younger."

Fanning.

"Kind words for sure but wasn't much more the bayou could teach her. She went to live with her brother in Houston. Nice family. They took care of her."

"Fortunate for her," Les said.

"She would spend part of the summers here with me, exploring the bayous. Became just like her papa. On occasion, she would bring up tourists, environmentalists. Show them the beauty of this place; give them a healthy respect for this God-forsaken part of His vineyard."

"So, her brother got her into college and graduate school?"

"She got some scholarships. An intelligent young woman she is. She had a benefactor, Mr. Michaels. Put her through all her learning. Paid her way. She didn't have to worry about money. Was all taken care of."

"You know who the benefactor was?"

"No one shared that with me. On her summer visits, Roxie would show me the Congratulations cards she got every year. I felt it was not my place to pry, you know."

"And how is she doing these days?"

Eugenie didn't reply immediately. She paused to hear a familiar noise. "Well, Mr. Michaels, I shall leave that up to you. I hear her pirogue now."

Eugenie and Les both arose. Rudy ran past them outside to the dock. No need for him to bark. He knew who was coming.

Chapter Twenty-Six – Les and Roxie

Roxie Cormier came down the Douillard channel and moored her boat just past Boudin's pirogue. She was surprised to see another man standing next to the dock with her old friend.

"You have a gentleman suitor, Miss Douillard?" Roxie asked. "Is this a bad time?"

"No, child. Thirty years ago. Maybe. He is here to see you."

Les reached out his hand to help Roxie onto the dock. "Lester Michaels, FBI, St. Louis office."

Roxie shook his hand firmly with a concerned look on her face. "I am on vacation for another week," she said. "Come back then."

Eugenie scolded the young woman. "Roxie, your manners."

"Sorry, Miss Douillard." To Les, she said.. "Please accept my apologies to you and to the agency. They know I am on vacation. I promise to be back on duty in 10 days."

"Pei Leung."

"Merde."

"Miss Roxanne. Language!" Eugenie said. "Just because we are in the backwater, don't mean you can speak like a gator boy."

"I am sorry, Miss Douillard."

Roxie pulled herself up onto the dock and gave Eugenie a hug with her head buried in her shoulder. "Who is this guy?" Whispering.

Eugenie whispered back, "Speak to him yourself. He came all this way to see you. Plus, he brought honey."

Roxie smiled at Eugenie and turned toward Les "You brought honey? This is serious. You're not courting the lovely Miss Douillard. You mentioned Pei Leung. I guess we need to talk."

"Pei Leung?" Eugenie asked.

"Business," Roxie said.

"I guess Rudy and I shall make ourselves scarce. You two run along. Play nicely, and keep your distance, Mr. Michaels. She'll drop you before your little brain cells can fire up a 'What happened?'"

"Tae kwon do?" Les asked.

"Krav Maga, Wing Chun," Roxie replied.

"Crap."

"Language, Mr. Michaels," Eugenie shouted as she and Rudy walked down the channel.

Roxie led Les into Eugenie's house and into the kitchen. "Who said to bring honey?" Roxie asked.

"Moyes."

"That big Bluto," she said smiling. "Give him a hug for me when you get back."

"Not if I want to keep my ribcage intact."

"How many jars did he tell you to buy to come here?"

"Three."

"I only see two."

"Moyes has the third."

"*Couyon.*"

"What? I'm not down with the Cajun lingo."

"That's okay, Eugenie won't hear us."

"So, Agent Cormier dit Boucher. I suppose you are wondering why I came down here just to get you?"

"The honey? Just Cormier is fine."

"Too hard for people to say the whole name?"

"No, just plays hell with database fields. So, I dropped the other parts and kept the first."

"Where did the whole name come from?"

"Old French family construct. Cormier was the family name. Dit Boucher is an alias. Sometimes references a profession or a location. Boucher means butcher. Cormier means a kind of tree. Although I like the Boucher better."

"Impressive."

"But we are not here for a genealogy lesson, are we?"

"No, Roxanne. We aren't."

"Call me Roxie. And speaking of names, you dropped Pei Leung like I had my net out ready to catch that. What gives?"

"I knew a name like that would not be something you would forget."

"No, Agent Michaels. Not that one."

"Call me Les. Seems like we have a pattern of killings like Pei's."

"Serial."

"Maybe. That is why you were called in."

"I have fifteen troubled kids and a few chaperones coming in a few days. I can't walk away."

"Shouldn't they still be in school?"

"These kids are lucky to be coming. The school board says they attend, or they don't move on to the next grade."

"I understand. Look, I'd like to say that I can hold off a week to ten days, but when you see the cases, it may change your mind."

"Agent Michaels, I don't need any more guilt trips in my life. I have enough to last me a while. I will see what I can do."

"That is all I ask."

"Best you get back to home base. Not the best place to have to spend the night and by the looks of it, old man Boudin won't be happy if he has to come looking for his boat. Anyway, I have more work to do before it gets dark."

"Need any help?"

"You brought honey. That is all you can do for us now. I must go. I am sure your GPS will get you back down to 307.

"I can manage, Roxie."

"Things change here, Agent Michaels. The sun casts shadows making shapes look different throughout the day. You have to be ever watchful."

With that last piece of advice, she was gone, in her boat and back out into the main channel.

Eugenie walked up to Michaels as he stared at Roxie boating off. "Quite something, huh, that child."

"She is not a child. She is um, well, I don't know."

"How about a woman. And not one to handle lightly."

"Like nitro glycerin."

"She can be explosive, but the bayou keeps her calm."

"And no man in her life?"

"As a lady, Mr. Michaels, I would not see fit to share in her delights."

"An enigma, for sure."

"You are beginning to see, Mr. Michaels, beginning to see. Keep to the center of the channel on your way back. Mr. Boudin will want his boat back before nightfall."

"I never mentioned it was his boat."

"Sir, you didn't have to. Everyone here knows everything about everyone else, except what should only stay here."

"Meaning?"

"Good day, sir. And merci for the honey. It was a kind gesture. Too bad it was a payment to get to Roxie, but then again, we all benefit from one another's situations."

"One more question before I go?"

"Your choice, Mr. Michaels."

"Roxie mentioned something about not needing any more guilts trips. What did she do that she has guilt?"

"Oh, my, my, poor child. All these years, and it still digs at her."

"Miss Douillard, if I am out of bounds, please say so, but if it helps me understand her better, I would like to know."

"Roxie has guilt because she could not get her father back to medical aid in time when he was bitten by that moccasin, as I had mentioned earlier. She panicked and got confused in the bayou. Couldn't find her way back. She lost focus at the worst time in her life. The time lost resulted in losing her father, whom she loved and respected. He was all she had, and she let him down."

"A lot of baggage to carry throughout her life."

"That is why she kept coming back every year. The bayou would never again beat her, and she thought being a part of it and knowing its every nook and cranny would help her over her pain of guilt. I guess she is still holding on."

"Well, I will keep all this in mind. I guess this is something I can take with me out of the bayou?"

"If you so desire. If you think it will heal her."

"You are a true lady, Miss Douillard. It was a pleasure."

He reached out to shake her hand, but she turned it over with palm down. A simple gesture not being lost on Les. He slowly bent over to kiss her hand.

"Good day, sir."

"Good day, Miss Douillard. If only I were thirty years older."

"Oh, my," she said, blushing and fanning.

Chapter Twenty-Seven – Benefactor

Night was slowly approaching as Roxie tied up the pirogue. Eugenie did not walk out to the dock to meet her or help with the lines. Roxie was tired after a long day of preparing the campsite for the kids coming next week. She loved this time off. Despite her workload back at the office, being in the backwater revived her.

"Eugenie, you in here?" Roxie asked.

"Here, Rochie. In the living room."

"Been a while since anyone called me Rochie."

"Been a while since old memories were conjured up. How was the visit with Agent Michaels?"

"The office needs me back."

"Something about a girl named Pei Leung, sparked some emotions in you."

"He didn't need to bring up business in front of you. It was not polite."

"Perhaps not, but does Pei need you?"

"Pei is dead."

"Oh my, child. I didn't know. How truly sad. Maybe her parents need you for their daughter."

"Her parents couldn't handle the grief. They went back to their home in China. Never returned."

"Why was she so important for you, then?"

"She was my first case. They wanted my take on some patterns found at the crime scene. Being a criminal behaviorist, they thought I could help."

"You never mention your cases to me, Rochie. Perhaps it is for the better."

"We leave some things to stay in the bayou, Eugenie. Some things need to stay out of it also. What I see doesn't belong here. And it is Roxie now. Pere Remy only called me Rochie."

"I'm sorry. I didn't mean to—"

"I have moved on," Roxie interrupted.

"You sure?"

"What do you mean?"

"Agent Michaels seems to think you are still hanging on to the guilt about Remy and the moccasin."

"Well, Agent Michaels needs to keep his business professional."

"I hope you are not upset with me that I mentioned it to him."

"Like I said, I have moved on."

"Right, Cher. So, will you go back to work or stay here?"

"What about the kids?"

"We don't need no city folk coming down here traipsing through the swamps trying to make themselves better in just one week."

"Are you saying that my work here for the past three years is useless?"

"No, child. You have done wonders for them all. We get the letters of gratefulness all the time. You just can't fix every child with a troubled spirit. It is the parent's job."

"But they aren't doing their job."

"Maybe next year, you bring the parents down here. Let them on their own for a week and say they can go home when they are ready to train their children proper."

A smile came across Roxie's face thinking it was a brilliant idea.

Eugenie added, "In fact, another person sent us a letter of thanks just the other day. I was going to show it to you when had the time."

"Did you already read it?"

"Oh yes, Cher. It is in the top drawer of the desk in the bedroom. Go in and read it. I will make us some lemonade, with a touch of that honey that Agent Michaels brought us."

"Splendid idea. Be right back."

Eugenie got up to go into the kitchen, and Roxie went into the bedroom to fetch the letter. As she approached the desk, Roxie remembered there were two top drawers one left and right. Being mannerly, Roxie thought it polite to not yell into the kitchen, so she picked one of the drawers on the right.

In it were documents Roxie had never seen, not that she would ever rummage through Eugenie's drawers, but these were school records. Roxie's school records, back through all the semesters as LSU, plus the ones from Northwestern. School transcripts, letters from admissions and finance, letters of progress from her time in school. She picked up a few papers and walked into the kitchen.

As Roxie entered, Eugenie looked up in surprise. "Oh my, child. I think you opened the wrong drawer."

"Eugenie, please explain this. These are my school records. Documents that I have never seen. Where did these come from? Did my brother send these to you?"

"Sit down, please."

"I think I will stand."

Roxie's stance prompted Eugenie to give one of those "You mind your elders" look. Eugenie said nothing. She just folded her arms waiting for Roxie to respond. And like the obedient Rudy, Roxie slow sat down in the chair opposite from Eugenie.

"Explain, please."

Eugenie began. "Please don't hate me, Cher. This was between your father and me, although he never knew about it.

Roxie was incredulous. "Miss Douillard, what does this all have to do with Papa and you? You two weren't lovers or something and you both squirreled away money on the side?"

Eugenie rose up and stood defiant. "Absolutement non. I would never do such a thing. Your father was a gentleman. He treated me as such."

"Then what the hell was this all about?"

"Some things just stay in the bayou, Cher."

"Not this. If it happened in the bayou, then I want to know. This is the bayou. We are the bayou. What happened?" Roxie started getting that cayenne in her again.

"Hmm, I figured you would eventually find out, child. I guess now is the time."

"Eugenie, this is not telling me about the birds and the bees and giving me that talk about a young girl growing to be a woman. I am a woman and need to know."

"Yes, yes. You are right, dear. Where shall we start?"

"How about the beginning?"

"Oh my. So many memories."

There was a moment of silence while Roxie waited for Eugenie to collect her thoughts. Roxie placed Eugenie's hands in hers to comfort the worried old woman.

"You remember my husband Charles? God rest his soul."

"Yes. Such a tragedy," Roxie said trying to calm down.

"They only found half of him washed on the shore. Charles was a big man. I guess the gator that got him, thought he was too much for one meal. You know he was an engineer," explained Eugenie.

"Yes, vaguely. Did research for the military."

"Yes, well, Charles sold a patent for some bearing machine to the government. He received a lot of money, more than we ever imagined."

"You mean you're rich?"

"As they say on TV, filthy rich."

"Jesus, Mary, and Joseph."

"Language, child."

"Cheeses, then. Eugenie all this time you are swimming in cash. Why are you still here? You can have some haute condo in Mobile along the beach and give up this thick air and fetid water."

"My life is here, Roxie. You know that. I would feel like I let Charles down if I left here and became city folk. Wouldn't be right."

"Mon Dieu. Incroyable. So, you have been my benefactor all this time? All these years? Getting me through school?"

Eugenie penitently lowered her head. "Yes."

Roxie started crying. "I didn't know. Didn't think I would ever know. Eugenie, why?"

"Your father did me a favor shortly before he passed."

"What did he do?"

"I do not know the particulars, and I am telling you the honest truth. I had some problems with some tourists one day. Later he told me he said I was safe. I assumed that he fixed the problem. I do not know what he did. He never got the chance to explain. The moccasin got him before I could repay the favor. So, I turned the favor to you without you knowing."

"I don't know what to say."

"I knew you needed a better life than what this place offers. It was my way of returning the favor to Remy."

"My schooling went into the thousands of dollars, with tuition, housing, everything."

"It went into way more than that, and now look at you. It has paid off. Every single penny."

"What about your sons? What did they get? Anything?"

"Who comes to see me every year, Cher? Who brings me honey? My sons have given up the backwater for places like Denver and Phoenix. Only you come back."

"This is all unbelievable. And you and my father never—"

"Arretez! Your father tipped his hat to me. That is all. His last words to me were 'I like you, Miss Eugenie'. Those words I shall never forget. Still get those freezons when I think of him."

"I told him to say that."

"Well, isn't that a lagniappe. Why?"

"Eugenie, he liked you, a lot, but he was a shy man and never thought he was good enough for you. He never knew about the money?"

"Money just corrupts people. He never knew. I guess if he found out, he would stop bringing me honey. Figured I could afford my own."

"Some things just stay in the bayou."

"Mais oui, Cher. Mais oui."

"I don't know how to repay you for all your kindness toward me, Miss Douillard. I don't know where to even begin."

"Can you do me a favor?"

"Another Cormier helping a Douillard?"

"But of course."

"Honey?"

"Always, ma Cher. There is another femme who needs you now. Pei Leung."

"But she is—"

"Is asking you to find her killer. Get your things. You can leave tomorrow."

"But the kids?"

"The little pansy-ass momma's boys can fend for they selves for another year."

"Miss Douillard! Language. Now, who's getting the cayenne in them?"

"I am a lady, for sure, but sometimes the lady has to let her hair down."

"Well, I never—" Roxie started to cry. She got up and walked over to Eugenie and gave her a big hug.

"How bout we have some Maque Choux, and call it a night?" Eugenie asked.

"Bien sur, Madame. We do it."

Chapter Twenty-Eight – Whiteboard

When Roxie arrived in the St. Louis Office, Les had already posted names of the victims on the whiteboard. There were pictures, personal information, cause of death, and location.

#1 Pei Leung 4/1/2010
#2 Wendy Stern 1/24/2013
#3 Annie Rhodes 11/11/2015
#4 Jennifer France 7/14/2016
#5 Ginger Tervil 3/29/2017

Les began running through the commonalities. "All died of severe trauma to the throat. None was sexually assaulted. All were found with semen on their bodies, postmortem."

"Pei was the first," Roxie sad quietly.

"Yes," said Les. "By the dates, it is obvious."

"No. I meant she was my first."

A deep sadness had come over her. Not knowing there were other women out there whom she could have saved, if only she had tracked down Pei's killer.

"You didn't know. Data was not shared with us. And there are things we still don't know."

"Like, are these women connected?" Roxie's sadness was turning to rage. "Were they all single?"

"Let's see. Well, no. Pei was single. Annie was a single mother. Wendy and Ginger were married."

"And they were all found or lived in various parts of the Midwest," Roxie added, reading the data sheets. "They all went to different universities, all majored in some technical field dealing with math in some variety. They were not found near the place where they lived. Except maybe Pei."

"So, you think they were abducted and driven to a specific location? Most seem remote."

"If we can find the pattern, then we might be able to find the killer."

Officer Sharp poked his head into the investigation room where Roxie and Les were going over the timelines on the board.

"Agent Cormier, I hate to interrupt," Sharp said.

"You have news on the case?" she asked.

"No, but I need you to come out here."

"Can it wait?"

Looking back down the hall and then to Roxie he said, "Yes. But we have a little problem."

Roxie put down her papers, slightly annoyed at the distraction. As she walked out the door and headed down the hall, she saw the source of Sharp's problem: Odie Lanham.

"What seems to be the problem?" she asked.

"Well, we heard that you were good with troubled kids," Sharp said. "Odie Lanham is one of them."

Expressing a sigh and then putting on her "nice girl" smile, she walked toward Odie.

"I can take it from here, Jeff."

"Knew you would."

Sharp decided to take another route to his desk. He didn't want to have to see Roxie confront someone that Sharp's office had dealt with a gazillion times.

Odie had his head down, one hand shackled to the bench. He didn't notice Roxie coming down the hall and sitting next to him. He was busy counting on his fingers and muttering to himself.

"1, 2, 4, 9, 16, 25."

Roxie put her hand on his free hand, and Odie stopped counting. Slowly he looked up toward a new face. When he saw her gentle smile staring at the handcuffs, a huge grin came over his previously sad and gloomy countenance. But his smile quickly retreated.

"Odie, my name is Roxie."

"I'm sorry. I just wanted to straighten things out, and he wouldn't let me," Odie said repentantly.

"Who is he, Odie?"

"The manager at the convenience store," he said.

"Odie, you know they have people who do that."

Odie's face became a little red, not from embarrassment, but from a tinge of anger.

"Yes. But they don't do it right. There has to be an order. An order."

Odie hung his head back down and started counting.

"36, 49, 64."

She sat there pondering the dilemma with Odie. *This was a gentle soul*, she thought.

Odekirk Roy Lanham was a high functioning autistic. The world was just not able to contain people like him. Yet God, Roxie thought, put him on this earth, so we could all be a little humbler.

Some people see God in a flower or the mountains. Roxie saw God in people like Odie. Most people didn't understand God, and they didn't understand Odie Lanham. Odie knew order. He knew the relationships between things and numbers. He counted a lot. He counted everything. This order saved him from a world of chaos and disorder. It also got him into trouble.

It was not the first time Odie was arrested for disrupting some business owner by straightening things, ordering things. To them, he was a nuisance and had to be removed. Instead of seeing his gift, they saw him as bad for business.

Odie's parents gave him up at the age of six. They didn't know how to handle him. He was the typical out of control kid left to the authorities to bounce in and out of foster homes until he turned sixteen.

Then he landed at the home of George and Suzanne Lanham, carrying with him sealed court records, poorly healed bones, and a troubled soul. George was an engineer. Suzanne was a Teacher. There were no other children in the home. It was never decided which of the two was unable to reproduce. It didn't matter anymore. Odie was adopted and the long arduous work of reformatting this human being began.

The Lanhams recognized that Odie had a penchant for order and as George pointed out, there is no better order than in numbers, plenty of them.

A few years and burdening weights of tears and struggles later, Odie was able to be on his own, somewhat. He tried a few jobs where his "skills" could be used, but the lack of social graces was too much for him. He could handle a Mersenne Prime. A relationship with humanity? Not so much. Fortunately, he still had George and Suzanne. Now he had Roxie.

Roxie put her hand under his chin and moved his head up for him to see her. There was only one thing she could do for him.

"Odie, you are a fine straightener," she said lovingly. "You make us all look really bad, because we just don't get it, like you do."

A tear came down his cheek. "But Miss Roxie."

"Never mind them. I will have a talk with them. We can fix this," she advised. Roxie motioned the attending officer to remove Odie's handcuffs. "I will take it from here, Officer."

"Are you sure you don't mind, Agent Cormier?" he asked.

"Odie's a good kid. We just need to find the right niche for him."

The officer removed Odie's cuffs as Odie rubbed his wrists. It was a pattern he was getting used to, and not a pattern he wanted to continue.

"Thank you, Sir, and to you, Miss Roxie," Odie said humbly.

The officer looked at Roxie and asked. "Will you take him home?"

"Do I have a choice?" she asked. "You know I will. I will find out where he lives, and we can have a little chat on the way."

Roxie took Odie by the arm and lifted him up. "I will take you home, but can you wait a few minutes?" Roxie asked.

"Yes, Miss Roxie. I will keep quiet," he replied.

They walked together down the hall to the investigation room, Odie counting the outlets, tile squares, and light bulbs all the way. As they entered the investigation room, Roxie pointed Odie to her borrowed desk.

"Odie, sit here for a little while and get out one of my puzzles on my desk."

Roxie always had a diversionary tactic for situations like this. Odie slowly picked up the stack and pulled out a word finder puzzle.

"Hi, Odie," Les said, smiling. "My name is Les."

"Hello, Officer Les," Odie replied, not looking up.

"Odie," Roxie said gently. "Some manners here."

Odie slowly raised his head and said "Yes, Miss Ro—"

That was all that came from his mouth. He looked past Les and became fixated on the white board.

There was an unsettled quiet in the room. Neither Les nor Roxie wanted to interrupt. Something stole Odie's attention. They noticed Odie's lips moving. He was mouthing something, but he was too quiet to hear.

"That is a nice puzzle," said Odie, breaking the silence.

Les and Roxie turned to the whiteboard. They saw nothing but what they put up there. Just some dates and names. No morbid crime scene photos. Nothing that would cause Odie any bother. A big smile came over Odie as he got up and walked toward the whiteboard. Roxie said nothing but motioned to Les to step aside. Odie planted himself right in the center of the whiteboard studying the data scrawled on it.

"Yes, Odie. A puzzle just for you," Roxie said. "Tell us what you see," Roxie shrugged her shoulders toward Les. Les shrugged back.

"Something will happen tomorrow on the 17th. What is it?" Odie asked.

Roxie was scratching her head at the "puzzle". "Odie, we don't get puzzles like you can solve, so please tell us what you mean. Tomorrow hasn't happened yet, so we don't know."

Odie stared at the whiteboard.

"May I draw on it, Miss Roxie?" Odie asked.

Roxie raced over and handed this not-for-this-world young man a red marker.

"Go ahead, Mr. Lanham, uh, Officer Lanham."

"Officer Lanham? I like Officer Lanham. Officer Lanham."

Over each date listed Odie wrote some numbers and a letter. He drew lines and wrote May 17 over to the right.

"Numbers and letter and lines, oh my." replied Les.

"This is not Kansas." Odie said sternly. "This is a date puzzle, and something will happen on the 17th."

"Odie, please tell us what you wrote and why the 17th?" Roxie asked.

"Numbers, Miss Roxie. Look. Between 1 and 2 is 34 months. Between 2 and 3 is 34 months. Between 3 and 4 is 8 months. Between 4 and 5 is 8 months."

Odie stopped talking and stared at the dates on the board. Les was about to speak, but Roxie waved him off. She didn't want to break Odie's concentration.

Odie then erased a few dates and replaced them with the day before. "These were wrong. Wrong dates. Bad dates. Bad monkey."

"But Odie, you can't cha—" Les said.

"Hush. Let the kid finish," said Roxie interrupting.

"Looks like the times are getting closer," Les whispered to Roxie.

"Some dates are missing," Odie said.

"Where?" Roxie asked.

Odie wrote more dates on the whiteboard.

October 29, 2014. December 17, 2016.

"This is better." Odie said. "The puzzle works now. You didn't give me the other two dates. Maybe you were testing me. Did I pass?"

Roxie looked at Les and shrugged. They were both standing behind Odie, but he didn't see them.

"Impressive, Mr. Lanham," Les said. "You did solve the puzzle, so where—"

"Wait. Puzzle not done." Odie interrupted as he wrote more dates on the board.

May17, June 7, July 5, July 19.

"There. Done," Odie said beaming. He turned around to see the other agents in a stupor, and a crowd had formed at the door watching this amazing person working his brain.

"Tell us what you see, Odie," Roxie said.

"Look, Miss Roxie. All these days are prime numbers. All these happened on a Wednesday. The next Wednesday with a prime number is the 17th. The puzzle says Number 6 is on the 17th. The 17th. Wednesday 17th. Tomorrow."

"Impressive, Odie," remarked Les. "But how do you know the dates in between?"

"Fido's Nachos," said Odie with a slight chuckle.

"The Fibonacci Number Sequence," shouted one of the officers standing in the doorway watching the young man solve a puzzle, no one could."

"But in reverse order," exclaimed Roxie.

"I like Fido's Nachos better," Odie said smiling.

Roxie got up and stood next to Odie, who was still enthralled with the whiteboard. She placed her hand on the young man.

"Odie, if we find out what happens tomorrow and everything is okay, we might just make you an officer like us," Roxie said. "Les, get in contact with the MEs who autopsied 1, 2, and 4 and see if there is a chance that time of death was before midnight."

"I'm on it."

Odie turned toward Roxie with a gleam in his eye. "Really? An officer?"

"Yes. It may be that you are the only one who could solve this puzzle. Maybe we'll make you the Mayor of Puzzleville."

Odie laughed. "You're funning me. There is no Puzzleville, Miss Roxie."

"Well, Odie. There should be. And you should be the Mayor."

"I think I will stick with Word Finders," he replied sadly. "No one will vote for me."

"Well, you have two votes from us," Roxie said.

A cheer went up from the people watching from the door, and more collected in the hallway. Odie saw them and beamed with joy that, for once, he could help someone.

"Looks like the whole building will vote for you, Odie. We need to get you home, Mayor Lanham. Your parents will be proud."

Blushing like a tomato, Odie grinned. "They will. I have made something of myself today."

"And every day from now on," Roxie said.

Chapter Twenty-Nine – Job Offer

After a few signed papers and some sincere apologies, Roxie drove Odie home, stopping at the convenience store on the way. Odie stayed in the car while Roxie walked inside.

Roxie walked up to the cashier who was filing her nails and violently chewing her gum behind the bulletproof glass. It was a slow time of the day. There wasn't much to do but preen.

"Where is the manager?" Roxie asked.

The cashier just pointed to the back room, trying not to make eye contact or get out of rhythm chewing her gum. It didn't take much to notice the conditions of the shelves. There was little attention to detail.

Knocking on the manager's door, Roxie heard "Come in".

Roxie opened the door. There was the manager sitting at his cluttered desk poring over receipts. Bo was on his name tag. Seemed like Bo was his full name. The way he looked was as if he was not smart enough to have more than two letters in his name. Roxie did not bother to ask for something more proper.

"You the manager?"

"Yeah. You are?" the manager asked.

"Agent Cormier, FBI."

"Not a social call, I see. Is it about the straightener? I warned him, and I will warn you. I don't want him in my store anymore. He is a disruption. Got it?"

The manager went back to his receipts.

Roxie slammed the door, causing Bo to jump up and spill his soda all over his receipts.

"Damn! Look what you did. What the hell was that for?"

Bo said, sopping up soaked pieces of paper.

"Bo, is it?"

Bo stood up and got too close into Roxie's face. He had to look up to her. That probably made him mad even more.

"Get out of my store."

Roxie pushed the manager back into his chair and leaned on the armrests. Now she was in his face, and he was frozen in a look of surprise.

"Look, Mr. Bo. I am here about Odie Lanham, the one you call the straightener."

"That psycho kid is not welcome here."

"I beg to differ with you. Not only will he be welcome in this store, you will offer him a job."

"What? You're as crazy as he is."

"I saw how filthy and rundown this place is. I see how the shelves are a mess. Why would anyone want to shop here?"

"Well, they do, and you're insane if you think I am going to give him a job."

"Well, Mr. Bo. Kindly accept my offer and I will promise not to call in my friends at OSHA, FDA, FCC, and the Health department. They would love to run their white gloves all over this place."

Bo didn't pick up on the FCC reference. The acronym had more letters than his name.

"This sounds like blackmail and extortion. You're trying to shake me down. I ain't hiding anything."

"You have thirty seconds." Roxie said as she pulled out her phone.

"Wait! He ain't working full time, no benefits."

Roxie started punching some numbers.

"Alright. He can come in and straighten things up. I admit that things are a little out of place. But that's all he can do. Three time a week."

"Four." Touching more numbers.

"Alright, alright."

Bo could hear Roxie calling someone on the other end.

"This is Les."

"I'm on my way. Had to make a stop."

"Come on, Agent. I don't need any more problems."

"What, Mr. Bo. You have more problems than I?"

"Um, no. Uh, I mean no. The kid. I mean, Odie can work here and keep things neat, starting tomorrow. Will that work?"

"Well, isn't that nice of you, Mr. Bo." Roxie replied. "And to make sure he does well, I will stop by on occasion to see how things are progressing. Give it a personal touch. How about that?"

"Yeah, whatever you say. I don't want trouble."

"Trust me. You won't. Not from me. Good day."

Roxie backed off and softly opened the door and gave the manager a curt smile, as she walked out. The manager turned back to his stained receipts and yelled out at the girl behind the counter.

"Liz, get your butt in here."

As Roxie walked past the nervous cashier, Liz gave her the evil eye.

"What the hell did you do?" she asked.

Roxie said nothing but smiled and left the store.

"Everything okay in there, Miss Roxie?" asked Odie.

"You have a job there starting tomorrow."

"Wow! Doing what?"

"What you do best, Mr. Lanham. They have an opening for a straightener."

"I didn't see any sign?"

"One just opened up. Aren't you lucky!"

The drive home was quiet. Odie went back to counting, but there could not have been a bigger smile on anyone in the whole world that day. If a prize were to be given out, Odie would have received top honors. George and Suzanne were told of the puzzle and the new job. They didn't seem like they fully understood, but they nodded to him in amazement and acceptance.

"We are proud of you, son," George Lanham said. "We knew you could make a difference."

Odie would be the hero. Little did he know how much.

Roxie hurried back to the office and to the puzzle. Les was still in the investigation room, adding more notes to the whiteboard.

"We have a math whiz serial killer." She said to Les.

"Wednesday's child is full of woe." he replied.

"You think he was born on a Wednesday?"

"I would bet a beignet on it," she said. "Let's see if we can pick this up in the morning. Maybe with a fresh set of brain cells."

"But if Odie's right about tomorrow, shouldn't we do something?"

"Hard to predict the future. Maybe we need a break for a bit."

"Agreed. Do you think we need Odie again?" Les asked.

"I hope not." Roxie said. "We don't need his delicate nature involved in these murders."

"Dinner?" Les asked. "St. Louis ribs?"

"Italian on the Hill," Roxie replied.

"Works for me. Isn't this your first time in St. Louis? How did you know about the Hill?"

"I'm a tracker, Les," she replied. "I can hunt down a good place to eat just as easily as a murderer."

Chapter Thirty – The Puzzle Revisited

The following day Les had come into the office early to figure out a connection to all the murders facing him on the whiteboard. Something was still missing, and they had very little time to come up with the clue as to who and when. Could the FBI trust in a young man who didn't fit in this world? They really didn't have a choice.

Roxie showed up around nine with coffee and an assortment of pastries from the café around the corner. Les noticed that she had not had much sleep the night before.

"Roxie, you look rode hard and put away wet," he said scanning her disheveled appearance.

"The Pasta a Vongole did not go well with me." Roxie replied. "It also did not help picturing those names on the board in my head all night."

"Take notes, then," Les advised. "Then the words can be on paper, and not in your head."

Roxie looked at him, wishing she could explain why she stopped taking notes when she was thirteen. He did not need to know; she was in no mood to share.

"I remember everything I see."

"So, do you remember where we were yesterday?"

"May 17. Today. Plus, according to Odie, we have two missing dates."

"You know, that's right. Most disturbing."

Both agents sat silently for a few minutes drinking down coffee and pondering who was missing. Were there two more victims that escaped their notice?"

"I have an idea," Les said.

"Anything will help at this moment," Roxie replied. "What is it?"

"Odie did dates. Do you think he can also do locations?"

"We could get the IT guys to run some analysis for us to come up with a pattern."

Roxie walked up to the whiteboard and picked up a marker.

"Let's think like Odie, shall we?"

"Sure, what do you have in mind?"

"We need a map," Roxie said, looking around the office for one.

"Google Earth," Les said as he walked over to a desktop.

"Let's look at each location and see if we can find a pattern."

"Okay," Roxie said with added hope. "I will call out the locations where they were found, and you can plot them."

"Give me a second to log in, and then we can do this," Les said as he worked the computer. "Okay, first location."

"Number 1, Memphis, Tennessee."
"Number 2, Armington, Illinois."
"Number 3, Creston, Iowa."
"Number 4, Beaver, Oklahoma."
"Number 5, Barnhart, Texas."

Les entered the locations onto the map. A pattern seemed to be forming. "It looks like a circle," he said. "Going in a counter-clockwise direction."

"But according to Odie, there are two places missing," Roxie commented as she saw Les' dots on the screen.

"Maybe the circle would be more rounded with those missing dots."

"There is also a lot of space between those dots," Les said. "Call the IT guys?"

Roxie pondered the moment. "Let's put in the exact coordinates of where they were found."

"Ready," said Les.

"Number 1, 35.086 N. 89.988 W."
"Number 2, 40.325 N. 89.282 W."
"Number 3, 41.0858 N 94.508 W."
"Number 4, 36.543 N 100.451 W.
"Number 5, 31.263 N 101.163 W."

"Got them entered. Hmm."

"What do you see?" Roxie asked.

"Just tighter points on a map."

"Odie."

"What about him?" Les asked as he swiveled around to Roxie.

"The kid sees things we don't. He sees patterns and data between them. He may be able to help with the missing dates or persons or locations, whatever they are."

"Do you know where he is?"

"I have a pretty good idea. Wanna come along?"

"You go. I'll see if I can work these coordinates some more. And I'll set up another whiteboard with just the locations on it for Odie."

"Be right back." Roxie got her jacket and called for a squad car with the most lights and loudest siren.

Chapter Thirty-One ~ The Straightener

Ten minutes later she pulled up in front of the convenience store lights going and siren wailing.

Bo the manager ran out the door. "What the hell. We didn't call 911."

"Is Odie here?" asked Roxie.

"Yeah, what is all this. Did he go screwing up someone else's store now?"

Roxie didn't reply. She ran past Bo and into the store. Odie was in the back along the dairy case. The first thing she noticed was that the place looked brand new. Everything was arranged in some pattern that only one young man could understand. And in less than a day, no less. When Odie saw Roxie out of breath standing in the aisle, a bright smile came over him.

"Miss Roxie. I am working," he said smiling.

"Unbelievable job, Mr. Lanham. I have never seen the store look so perfect."

"Yes. Mr. Bo gave me the job. He even made a badge just for me."

The manager came into the store behind Roxie and followed her into the aisle. "I hate to say it, but the kid did a good job on the place."

"All it took was a chance to see past his gifts, didn't it? And the badge thing? Nice touch, Bo."

"You were right, but what the hell is with all sirens and rushing?"

"Mr. Bo, the FBI requires the keen skills of Mr. Lanham at this moment."

The request was loud enough for Odie to hear. And made the manager chuckle. "What? The FBI is changing their name to BFI so the letters can be arranged alphabetically?"

Roxie smiled, but the joke was lost on Odie. He either didn't understand or thought they were making fun of him. His smile quickly departed.

Roxie looked over at Odie. "Officer Lanham, we need you to solve another puzzle. Please come with us."

The smile returned. As Roxie and Odie walked past the manager, he was astounded and just shook his head.

When they got into the police car, the manger hurried out the door. "You will bring him back, won't you? He is needed here," Bo said humbly.

"After we finish needing him."

"Full siren mode, Officer Lanham?"

"Full siren mode, Agent Roxie."

The police car carrying a special gift left as quickly as it came. The girl behind the counter looked out the window at the disturbance. She kept chewing her gum and doing her nails.

When Roxie and Odie returned to the investigation room, Les was ready with the extra whiteboard and requested data meticulously attached.

"Hello, Agent Les," Odie said proudly.

"Greetings, Mr. Lanham. I hear you're working at the convenience store."

"Officer Lanham to you. But just for today."

Les looked past Odie as Roxie was mouthing "just go with him."

Les gave Odie a smart salute. "Yes, of course. Officer Lanham, we have an important puzzle for you to solve. We are grateful for your help with the dates. Now we need a location where this thing will happen next week."

Odie didn't hear. Well, yes, he heard, but his brain had already gone to work.

Les whispered to Roxie as she walked up next to him. "He is like one of those guys in the movie *Dune*, a human supercomputer."

"He is just a kid with a gift, well okay, a super-computer gift."

"What do you see, Odie?"

"Miss Roxie, I don't know some of these places. Do you have a map?"

Les got up and ran into another room, retrieving a map of the U.S. "Here you go, Officer Lanham."

"Odie is my name. I'm not good enough to be an officer."

"Yet," Roxie finished. "Okay, Odie. Let's put dots on the map where all these places are."

Odie picked up a marker and began drawing dots. A three by three array of dots.

"Odie, what about these two places?" Les asked.

"Shhh. Let him finish," Roxie whispered.

"This is a fun puzzle, Miss Roxie. Draw four straight lines through all nines dots without going over the same dot twice and you can't take your pencil off."

"Did you say nine dots, Odie?" Roxie looked at Les.

"Yes, isn't that the game? The puzzle you wanted me to solve?"

Both Les and Roxie stood up. On a part of the whiteboard they tried to connect the nine dots with four straight lines. They could not figure out the way to do it.

"Okay. Watch," Odie said instructing. "You cannot solve this without going outside the nine dots. Outside the box. That is the only way to solve the puzzle. Outside the box, the dots."

Odie drew on the map with four straight lines through all nine dots, each only once, but the two places he did not originally touch did go outside the array and right over some place in Wisconsin, and the other place in a spot north of El Paso, Texas. Odie circled the bottom center dot.

"This is where tonight will happen."

"Odie, what about these other three?"

Odie drew a circle around the bottom right dot. "It will happen here next month on Wednesday the 7th."

He then drew a circle around the center dot. "This," he added, "will happen on Wednesday, July 5th."

On the upper left dot, he wrote Wednesday, July 19th.

"Are you sure?" Les asked.

"Agent Les, that is what the puzzle says. Puzzles don't lie. Only people lie."

"You have done a wonderful job. The FBI will be grateful to you, Mr. Lanham," Roxie said patting his shoulder.

"What's going to happen tonight at this place, Miss Roxie?"

Roxie looked over at Les not sure how much information to share. "Someone got lost, Odie. We think he will be there."

"I guess he likes puzzles and games, too, huh, Miss Roxie?"

"That he does." she was honest with Odie. There would be someone lost, but the game being played was dangerous, and played by a sick individual, someone who needed to be stopped.

Roxie called in an officer to have Odie returned to the store. As he was leaving the investigation room, Odie stopped. "I hope I helped you and Agent Les."

Roxie walked over to the young man and gave him a hug and a kiss on the forehead.

"More than you know, Mr. Lanham." The words of praise brought a smile to the young man's face. To the attending officer, Roxie said "He will show you where to take him. Make it with lots of lights and sirens."

"Yes, ma'am."

As the officer and the "special agent" departed, Les turned to Roxie. "You really are good with kids. The ones on your bayous excursions are lucky."

Roxie became somber with the weight of another murder on her hands. "We need to call Houston police. There will be or there may have already been a murder. Let's hope that we get there in time."

"And if it's too late?" Les asked.

"Then we have to save the last three. And get someone on the phone about the dot in Wisconsin and El Paso. Something happened there. I want to know what."

"Happened?" Les asked with an emphasis on the past tense. "You think a death or deaths have already occurred?"

"If Odie drew the solution correctly, then I have reason to think we will find something. And we can extrapolate the dates and may find a clearer picture."

"We're tracking down a sick individual."

"Who loves killing as a game."

"Speaking of pictures," Les said. "Let's go back to the shots at the crime scene. I remember the victims' positioning seemed contrived."

Les got out all the photos and lined them up in the same array as Odie's puzzle.

"Merde," Roxie said.

Les saw it also. The victims were oriented in a certain direction and are pointing to the next victim like big arrows.

"But look," Roxie exclaimed. "Victim 2 is pointing at the unknown place in Wisconsin. And Victim 4 is pointing toward El Paso."

"Victim 5 is pointing to the location for today," Les added. "The murderer had lined up his victims in a specific order. He knew them all and he planned it all from the beginning."

"Another thing, Les." Roxie scanned the locations from Google Earth. "All the bodies were either at or near an intersection."

"So, the body could be easily found, you think?"

"So, the game can be even more sick. Houston needs to be notified. Right away."

Chapter Thirty-Two ~ Position Eight

Stacy Eddings failed to show up at the office of the insurance agency where she worked as an actuary in the Galleria Area in Houston. She called in to her admin assistant at eight and said she was running behind, because a friend she was meeting for breakfast was late. There was no entry on her calendar.

Jeff Eddings, her husband, called the office at 9:30 asking about dinner plans after work. When Stacy's assistant said she had not arrived, Jeff immediately logged in to his computer and opened the Where's MY IPhone app.

Stacy had lost her phone once, and Jeff wanted to make sure the next phone would not get misplaced. He also knew it was a nice safety feature for living in a big city like Houston.

The app located the phone in Prairie View, northwest of Houston. He knew his wife had dealings with agents all over the city and surroundings areas. Not wanting to be over-protective, Jeff decided she was working, so he did not call. At noon, he thought his wife would be finished, so he called her. The phone rang four times and went to voicemail. This meant that the phone was still on. He went back to find phone app. It was now registering near the town of Anderson.

An hour later, he launched the app. No movement. He decided to wait another hour. Thirty minutes later the phone rang.

"Stacy, what the hell?" Jeff asked, with a worried voice.

"Mr. Eddings?" the voice on the phone asked.

"Who is this?"

"Sheriff Bivens, Grimes County Sheriff's Department. Your wife has been attacked. She is at Grimes St. Joseph Hospital in Navasota."

"What happened? Geez, I have been trying to reach her."

"We need you to get here as soon as possible."

"I'm in Spring. It will take an hour or more. Can you tell me what happened?"

"Mr. Eddings, all we can say is she has been brutally attacked. May have been raped. Please, hurry."

"I'm on my way. Tell her I'm coming."

"But, Mr. Eddings she—"

Too late to hear her condition, Jeff hung up the phone and raced out of the house towards Navasota and hour away.

Sheriff Bivens was waiting outside the emergency entrance when Jeff Eddings pulled up.

"Mr. Eddings?" Bivens asked.

"Where is my wife? Where is Stacy?" Jeff asked, pleading.

"I'm sorry, but your wife is in surgery. Her neck was severely crushed. They are working on her as we speak."

Jeff fell to his knees. "What happened?"

"Do you know why she would have been in Anderson?"

"No, I don't. What the hell happened?"

"We don't know for sure beyond getting kidnapped. She was found on the side of the road, brutally attacked. Why was she up there?"

"I don't know. Clients, maybe. She had a number in the Houston area, but she never mentioned Anderson."

"Did your wife have any dealings with the FBI?"

"This is crazy. Why the hell would she be messing with the FBI? She had private clients. What do you know?"

"We got a call from an office in St. Louis asking the Sheriff's Department to look for a murder to take place in the area where your wife was found."

"To take place? You mean you knew about this and didn't do anything?"

"Mr. Eddings, we had a chopper in the air scanning the area and the call came from a citizen driving past an intersection, saw her, and stopped to call 911. Our officers were faster than normal because of this warning from St. Louis."

"I have no idea what this is all about. Can I go up to see her now?"

"I'll have an officer show you up to a waiting area. Maybe we can get more information when she is out of surgery and she is awake."

An hour later, Stacy Eddings died from her wounds inflicted on her by a madman. The attacker's "gift" was left on her body, like the other victims, but just on her clothes. It may have been because killer had less time like the others. Perhaps he knew the police were getting close.

Bivens called the number that the FBI had given his department after he returned to the station.

"Agent Cormier," Roxie said picking up the phone.

"Agent Cormier, this is Sheriff Bivens of Grimes County in Anderson, Texas."

"I hope you have some good news for us, Sheriff."

"I wish I did, ma'am. Not sure how you knew this tragedy was going down, but we found the victim. We thought just in time. But I just got the word she didn't make it."

"This is most unfortunate, but thanks for getting someone out there quickly."

"If only sooner, ma'am."

"Sheriff, has the police report been done?"

"I will check with officer at the scene. Why may I ask?"

"Can you reach the person who found her and ask him in which direction she was lying and how she was lying?"

"An odd request, but I'm sure it is still in the Good Samaritan's mind. Let me call you back." The sheriff hung up.

"Victim Six did not make it," Roxie said sadly.

"Any word as to how he positioned her?"

"The sheriff is checking with the driver who stopped to help."

After a long wait and having the victim's information added to the whiteboard, the phone rang.

"FBI, Agent Michaels."

"Sheriff Bivens, Grimes County. You with Agent Cormier?"

"Yes, Sheriff. Any new information?"

"Tell her that the victim Stacy Eddings was lying flat on the ground, hands to her side, pointing east."

"Can you please give us the intersection where she was found?"

"What makes you think—" the Sheriff paused reviewing the notes, "The intersection of 2562 and 217."

"Do you have the victim's maiden name?"

"Um, let's see. Kaplan with a K."

"Thank you, Sheriff."

"Any way you can tell me what this is all about? How you knew this murder was going to happen and where?"

"Yes, I think your office has been of service to us. As soon as we figure out what is happening, we will tell you."

"Should I be expecting another murder?"

Les looked at the map of the 9 dots.

"No, Sir. You will not have to worry about another one, well, not in your area."

"That's good, because this one is like right out of the movies. The reality version of Minority Report."

Bivens hung up all the while thinking. *Where is Tom Cruise?"*

Les hung up and looked over at Roxie. "I hate to say this, but where is the next murder going to be?"

She walked over to the map and looked at where Odie's Number 9 dot was located.

"Mon Dieu, incroyable."

"Share?"

"The next place is in my backyard. The backwater, the bayous. We are not going to let him get away this time."

Roxie changed to an accent that she gave up long ago. "Hoo wee. We ain't gonna let no peeshwank come down here and mess with dis bayou, it gonna eat his ass up and spit dat boy out. Quest *couyon.*"

"But we have three weeks. You think the killer will up his schedule or change his place?"

"No way. This one is already got his mind made up and he ain't gonna let today mess up his game."

"Next step?"

"We need to find the other people on the list and try to understand why this is happening. We need to find out what happened in Wisconsin. The connection must be there."

"Sounds like it's time for a road trip?"

"Works for me."

Chapter Thirty-Three - Wisconsin

Roxie and Les got off their flight in Green Bay and had a rental car waiting for them. They were headed to Laona, Wisconsin, a small town about a hundred miles from the airport and seemingly far from the terrible world in which the two agents lived. Laona was away from everything. How could any place such as this be a key to unspeakable crimes?

Roxie had phoned ahead asking about any deaths, suspicious or not, that occurred on or about October 29, 2014 in the area. An affirmative was returned, thus prompting the trip. Roxie made sure the local authorities knew of their arrival. She was met by Sheriff Olander as they walked into the station.

"Agents Cormier and Michaels. Nice to meet you," Olander said.

"Sorry to have to meet under such circumstances, Sheriff," Roxie replied.

"Well, it is a surprise. We don't get many ABC organizations up here."

"So, you received our message. What did you come up with? Anything out of the ordinary?"

"Yes, actually. A few years ago, we investigated the death of a Shirley Johnson."

"What was the reason for an investigation?"

"She was in her late thirties. Her doctor said she was in excellent health for a woman her age. Home well kept. Maybe too well kept."

"Meaning?"

"You can see for yourselves when the warrant comes through. In the meantime, a little background on the Johnsons."

"Sure," Les said. "Whatever help you can give us. our only concern is that we're running out of time."

"Flight to catch?"

"I wish it were that easy. We have indications that there may be another victim in a serial murder."

"Damn. Okay. No time to see the sights then, huh?"

"Wish it were so. What can you tell us?"

"Elbert Fillmore and Shirley Johnson lived out in the county. On a few acres. Bobbie Lee, their son, comes along unplanned. Dad decides he is not going to play father and disappears. Left a note 'This wasn't what we agreed to.' Shirley never heard from him thereafter. Neighbors say it tore her up. Alone with a child, no prospect for a decent future."

"Was there ever a legal divorce?"

"There was never a legal marriage. She tried to find him for child support."

"Was she successful?"

"Got zilch. Only good thing for her was that she picked up the pieces in her life, put up a greenhouse with the help of some friends and sold quality produce from her home. Enough to keep her head above water."

"She was a little overprotective of her son. Right?"

"That poor boy was doomed from the beginning. She went extreme. Fearful, I guess, of losing him. But she went overboard."

"Wouldn't let him out of her sight," Les said.

"Exactly. Kid became anal retentive like her. He also became a genius, maybe his way of escaping his mother."

"Math and other academics?"

"Yeah. Some people at the schools nearby wanted him as a tutor at age ten. He was apparently good. Mom said no. Worried, I guess, that he would pick up some germ."

"Did Shirley have any relationships?"

"From what I hear? She hated men. Not that she turned to women. But after Elbert bounced, she went ice queen on any man who would show any interest."

"Probably drove her crazy raising a future 'man'."

"Good point."

"So, back to her death. What raised suspicions requiring an investigation?"

"Healthy woman falls down a flight of stairs, neck broken when she hits the bottom. Could have been pushed. Hell, if I were imprisoned by her, it would have been motive."

"You ruled out her son?"

"He had a number of witnesses saying he was at school in Green Bay. When he arrives back home, she is lying dead at the bottom of the stairs. Kid calls 911."

"Did the coroner give time of death?"

"Looks like she fell when the son was at school."

"Was this Bobbie Lee upset that his mother just died?"

"He could have been the next face on Mount Rush-more. Stone cold. No tears."

"Probably still in shock from losing his mother."

"Probably partied all night after her burial. Even though there seemed to have been motive, local authorities didn't press any charges. Wrote it off as an accident, act of God, bad luck, her time to go. Lucky break for the kid."

Olander's phone rang. "Yeah, Okay." He hung up. "We just got the warrant. Let's head on out."

Olander and the agents pulled up to the Johnson home. It was a simple dwelling, but meticulously groomed on the outside. Nothing seemed out of place.

"We have had a cruiser on the house all morning, no sign of anyone. No one came or left," said Olander.

"Standard entry procedure?" Roxie asked, pulling out her service revolver.

"I doubt anyone is inside. Let's try the front door."

"You're kidding," Les said.

"This is not New Orleans, Agent Cormier. People just don't lock their doors around here." Olander motioned to Les and Roxie to go in first. "After you."

The door was unlocked.

"Cheeses," Roxie said looking around surprised. "Look at this place. Spotless, No dust. Everything in order. Nothing out of place. Area rug perfectly centered in the room. I bet if you measured the distance between the edges of the rug and the walls, the values would match."

"No musty smell, no smell of any cleaners. Just a light fragrance of vanilla," Olander added.

"I smell it too. Bobbie Lee has not been gone too long."

"Sheriff, Roxie," Les said from the kitchen. "Look at this. What do you see?" The other two followed Les in.

"Kitchen utensils, knives, forks, spoons all lined up perfectly on the counter."

"Yes, but they are not aligned with the edge of the counter," said Olander.

"Seems like they are all pointing to specific direction."

"This is sick."

"Anal retentive," Roxie said, looking out the kitchen window.

"This is disturbing. The kid needs help."

"Well looks like everything is pointing out the window, to north. Mon Dieu, I think we also have a geo-location fanatic."

"A what?" Les asked.

"All those things in the kitchen are pointing north. The kid is a freak on geo positioning."

"What does that mean?" Olander asked.

"Our Bobbie Lee likes to point north and wants his whole world positioned accordingly," Roxie replied. "Almost as if his whole life needs to be anchored to something immovable."

"But if our Bobbie Lee is that good at math and celestial trigonometry, he knows that not even the north star is constant."

"The positioning of the bodies. He is playing some kind of game with us or with his victims."

"So, you think we have our killer?" Les asked.

"Sheriff, do you know if he was ever in any trouble with any of his friends?"

"Agent Cormier, he had no friends," replied Olander.

"Someone at school maybe?"

"Go up to the college and talk to some of his professors," Olander advised.

"Let's see where the mother fell."

They walked through the kitchen to the basement door and proceeded down the stairs.

Olander began, "We found her lying down here on her back. I can send you the photos taken when the coroner arrived on the scene."

"Nothing unusual about anything that you saw?" Les asked.

"None that jumped out, although it seemed to me that her final resting place was somewhat out of order compared to the stairs."

"Didn't the ME's office state the body was not moved?"

"Correct."

Roxie slowly walked up the stairs eyeing the carpet on the steps, feeling the railing. "Les, Sheriff. come up here."

"See something?" Les asked.

Roxie bent down at the top of the stairs. "Look at the place here about 4 inches above the top step."

"Looks like a simple nick to me."

"Same place, same height on the opposite side."

She took out a knife and gently scraped the area around the nick, revealing a small hole.

"He painted over the hole and one on the other side."

"I'll be damned. You're thinking trip wire?" Olander asked.

"Thin enough not to see, possibly held in by eye bolts," Roxie explained. "If you look on the downward side of the hole, you will see it seemed to be stretched out a little, like his mother caught the wire, and the eye bolt gave way a little, pushing out the hole."

"Then junior comes home, sees mommy dearest, removes the trip wire and bolts and carefully patches up the hole. No one noticed," Les added.

"Did the coroner notice any marks caused by the trip wire?"

"Many bruises on her legs, arms, and body from the fall," said Olander. "She was wearing garden boots at the time. Probably coming from the greenhouse."

"Where are her boots now?"

"No reason to have suspected foul play. Her belongings were returned to her son."

Les went out through the kitchen. "I'll look around to see if I can find the boots."

"In the meantime, Sheriff, can you have someone send me the photos taken by the coroner?"

"On it."

After a few minutes, Les walked back into the kitchen.

"Found the boots?" she asked.

"Like a good son, they were in the greenhouse neatly stored on a mud mat by the door," Les said.

"Any sign of wire marks on the toes?"

"Just above toe at ankle level on the right boot, you can see a slight defined line, could be caused by a wire. But the boots have seen their time in the garden."

"We can get the crime lab to put the boot under a scope."

Roxie to Olander. "On what date was the mother pronounced dead?"

Olander replied, "I have it here. Just a sec." Running through his notes. "October 29, 2014."

"Mon Dieu. Another Wednesday. Odie was right."

"What do you mean?" Olander asked.

"There was a specific pattern to the dates in question. Each woman was killed on a Wednesday. Then there was a two-year period, an empty space in the pattern. Two years sound like a round number, but the date was predicted by some calendar counting autistic man back in our office. Not only two years but 21 months passed, then the Johnson death then 13 months to the next murder."

"So, as part of this whole revenge thing, his mother was another date on the calendar?" Olander said. "Damn. This kid is sick."

"And he is going to kill again. Our source says in three weeks. Do you know when Bobbie Lee was born?"

Olander referred back to his noted. "Robert Johnson's DOB? Uh huh. Crap."

"Tell me he was born on a Wednesday."

"Do I even need to answer?"

"Wednesday's child is full of woe."

"I know the poem," Olander said. "Never thought it would be true."

"Neither did I," said Roxie, thinking to herself that was her birthday. Remembering the woe in her life: her dad. the moccasin, being lost. A cruel mother torturing a son with a brilliant mind. "You say the father is dead?"

Olander replied. "No one knows."

"So, he could still be alive."

"I suppose so."

"I think we should do a search to see if any Elbert Fillmore is in the system somewhere. I will get my people on it."

"Anything I can do, Agent Cormier?" Olander asked.

"Send the father's info, whatever you have or can get, to the office in St Louis. Which way is Bobbie Lee's room?"

"Up the stairs to the right, Olander pointed. You won't miss it."

Roxie and Les went upstairs to find Bobbie Lee's room. Olander was right. They didn't miss it. The room was immaculate. Everything was in order, aligned, oriented. Nothing out of place. They rummaged through his drawers, under the bed. A model son, model home.

"Les, let's take his laptop over there. We will see if he is meticulous in his writing," said Roxie.

"You think he took notes of his 'work'?" Les asked.

"I hope so for the sake of those he hasn't killed yet."

They found the mother's bedroom. Untouched. The bed was made. All the drawers were empty, closet empty. Bobbie Lee must have given away all her clothes. There were no pictures sitting or hanging. The room had not been disturbed since she had used it. It was just too sterile.

"Agent Cormier, come see this."

She walked back into Bobbie Lee's room where Olander was holding a stack of old letters. "Where did you find those?"

"I pulled out one of the drawers, and they were behind in the back."

Roxie took the letters and went downstairs to the dining room. She laid out all the letters and they started reading them.

"Well, isn't this interesting."

"Find something?"

"Looks like daddy got a conscience. There is a letter from him to Shirley, saying he was sorry."

"When was it dated?"

"About 2 months before her death."

"Bobbie Lee had the letters. This means he found out about his father."

"Where are the letters postmarked? El Paso?"

"Las Cruces, New Mexico, just up the inter-state."

"We need to find Bobbie Lee's father right away.

"Why?" asked Olander.

"We think bobby is going after his father or may already have."

"If he killed his mother, he will do his father in also. And if Odie is right, Mr. Fillmore is already dead."

"We need to call the El Paso office."

"Who is Odie?" Olander asked.

"Hard to explain Odie," Roxie replied. "But in a nutshell, he is somewhat like Bobbie Lee, bright like Bobbie Lee, but not violent."

"We need Bobbie Lee's vehicle information, and also his mother's just in case. Can you get that for us?"

"Already have it. Knew you would want it."

"We need to get back to Green Bay to see the kid's professor."

"Wait," Les said, reading another letter. "Listen to this."

"What now?"

"Perhaps sonny boy inherited some money from his grandparents on mother's side, so he has the means to get around to all his victims."

"So, that is why the mother stopped working. She didn't have to."

"But the money was only for Bobbie Lee. Her job was to spend it on his behalf."

"I can't imagine that went well."

"Maybe that was why she treated him the way she did."

"Punishment."

"Exactly."

The agents finished their investigation at the Johnson home, thanked officer Olander for his assistance, and headed back to Green Bay and to the university.

Chapter 34 – The Professor

At the University of Wisconsin at Green Bay, Roxie and Les found the building where the Math Department was housed. They waited outside Professor Khalid's office. Roxie stopped noticing how many times Les looked at his watch. Roxie moved into bayou mode. *Go slow like the backwater.*

When the bell sounded, students poured out of the classrooms. Eventually Professor Khalid approached the agents sitting in chairs by his door. They both stood up to greet the professor.

"Agents Cormier and Michaels. FBI. May we have a word?" Roxie asked.

Khalid replied, "Oh yes, of course. I am sorry you had to wait. I would have come earlier but my grad student got sick and I had to teach the class on simplex methods myself."

"That's fine, Professor," Roxie said. "Thank you for giving us some of your valuable time."

As they followed Khalid into his office he pointed to some chairs by his desk.

"Please sit. Now what is all this about. Has one of my students gotten him or herself into some trouble?"

"Bobbie Lee Johnson," Les said hurriedly.

"A name I haven't heard of in a while. Oh my. He was a brilliant young man. Surely he would not have done anything to harm anyone."

"Why do you say that, Professor?" she asked. "You knew him well, I assume."

"Oh yes a delightful young man. Shy. Didn't socialize much. People looked up to him and scorned him at the same time, because he was brilliant. People were jealous, but he was also untouchable. I heard he had a tough home life. Mother was overprotective. Then after she died, I didn't see him much."

"No friends? Not a member of any school clubs like chess or mathletes?"

"Oh no. Not Bobbie Lee. But—" Pondering.

"Yes, Professor?"

"Well, a few years ago, he was invited to Math Camp sponsored by our department in conjunction with a university in Missouri. He was asked to give a presentation on the Riemann Hypothesis."

"The what?"

"Oh, some unsolvable theorem something that we, as you put it, mathletes, have dangling in front of us like the carrot to a horse."

"What do you think made it so memorable then?"

"Something happened there, and when I asked Bobbie Lee about it, he got defensive and shut down any further discussion about his experience. I was hoping he would come back saying he solved it."

"And yet you don't know what happened?"

"I'm afraid not."

"Do you know anyone who might have attended Math Camp at the same time?"

"Actually, I do. My secretary would have that in her files. You may speak to her. I am sorry that I cannot be of more assistance, Agents, but I must get ready for my next class."

"You have been a great help, Professor."

"Bobbie Lee is not in any big trouble, I hope."

Roxie smiled the smile one gives to another when they don't want to share the truth. "We just want to find him to make sure that is not the case."

"Well, good luck to you."

When the agents left Professor Khalid's secretary, they carried a folder with a list of names from Math Camp. On their way to the airport, they opened it and began reading.

Roxie said, "Looks like there were a number of kids at the Math Camp." Then there was a pause. "Mon Dieu."

"What is it?"

"Listen to these names. Pei Leung, Stacy Kaplan, Jennifer Bishop, Wendy Stern, Ginger Tervil, Annie Rhodes and others."

"All of our victims. He is killing off people, girls from Math Camp. What women are not on our list?"

"Well, there were hundreds of kids there, so a lot of names. Wait. There is some code next to our victims' names. The letters ND."

"So, who else has ND next to them?" Les asked, secretly wishing Odie were there.

"Indira Patel, Carol Meyers, and Amanda Horsch."

"Get on the line to St. Louis and see if you can find where these women are."

Les called the office asking for information on the remaining women. By the time they got to the airport, Les got a reply by text.

"Okay. Here we go," Les said as he read off the information. "We found an Amanda Horsch in Limon, Colorado, Indira Patel, now married, last name Gamal, living in Boise, Idaho. No data on a Carol Meyers."

"Pick a name, and let's go talk to her," Roxie said.

"We also need to go to El Paso and find out what happened at the other outside point that Odie mentioned."

"Let's call the El Paso office and see if they have anyone there who can track down this Elbert Fillmore."

Les got back on his phone and dialed El Paso. Roxie heard him request data on Bobbie Lee's father and to have anything they can get be sent to his and Roxie's phones.

Roxie called the St Louis office requesting a BOLO for Bobbie Lee Johnson, starting with Texas and adjacent states. When she got off the phone, Roxie picked up the list of names.

"Indira is too far west. Let's give Amanda Horsch a visit. Ever been to Limon, Colorado?" she asked.

"I am glad I pack for changes in plans," said Les. "And yes, I have been to Limon. Well, you only really pass through Limon. There is no real reason to visit there."

Roxie called the Denver office and made arrangements for transportation and for any information they may have on Amanda Horsch.

Chapter Thirty-Five – Limon

Roxie and Les arrived at Denver International Airport. They were picked up by a local agent who drove them to the Denver office. When they arrived, the Section Chief, Avery Collins, called them into his office.

"We got your requests for information just a while ago," Collins said.

"Thanks for tracking this Amanda Horsch down for us," Roxie said.

"Limon is quite a distance to go tonight. Are you sure you don't want to crash in a hotel for the night and start fresh in the morning?"

"Were it that easy," Les said, wishing he could get a decent night's sleep.

"We have a deadline and need to speak with Ms. Horsch and get down to New Orleans."

"Suit yourself."

"How did you find Horsch? In Limon of all places? What's so exciting there?" Roxie asked.

"Nothing much in Limon but the truck stop where one of our state highway patrol officers had her name."

"Personal?"

"He wishes. No. She was cited for some disturbance a while back. Seems like she has a temper. Truck driver got in her face, and a bowl of chili got in his."

"And she didn't get fired?" asked Les.

"No." Collins explained. "The trucker was getting a little too frisky. The manager and some other customers saw the whole thing. It was a matter of self-defense."

"Assault with a deadly bowl of chili."

"I have been there. It's killer stuff. The trucker suffered some minor burns, and major embarrassment. The manager kindly asked him to move along."

"Do you mind if we take one of your vehicles out there?"

"Go right ahead, but on one condition."

"Bring back some chili?" Les asked.

"Yeah, but that stuff gives me serious heartburn," Collins said, hoping his stomach wasn't listening to the conversation. "Just the mild. I can only do it once a year if that, but they have corn bread you'd sell your mother for."

"Sounds like Limon is a dangerous place for foodies."

"Well, just be prepared for your visit with Miss Horsch. She's feisty."

"How do you know she is still there?"

"Verl, the manager would never let her go. She's good for business, you know. Always nice to have a looker behind the counter on those long roads, especially when you are in eastern Colorado and Kansas. I'll call down and they can have car ready in a short while."

"Much obliged, Chief Collins," Les said.

On the Colorado license plate there is an image of mountains. It does not speak to the Colorado east of Denver. If you stand on a tuna can, you can see Kansas. So, it wasn't hard to find the Limon truck stop on I-70.

It was also not hard to find Amanda Horsch when Roxie and Les walked into the diner. There she was like Collins said. A looker. Tall brunette, voluptuous, showing every curve that she could display legally. Roxie tried not to notice Les scanning her like all the other truckers going in and out of Verl's Diner.

Amanda was working the counter and was engaging those fortunate gents who found a seat there. So, Roxie and Les decided to take a booth.

"And to think she is a math genius under that uniform." Roxie said.

"Yes, um, that is why we are here. Correct?"

"Not for the chili."

Peggy the waitress came up behind them. Well, Peggy was the name on her badge. She was not the attention getter like the one working the counter. Maybe that was the reason for working the booths. She looked as if she had been working there since the last ice age scoured eastern Colorado and western Kansas.

"I heard chili. You want chili?" Peggy said. She noticed Les was admiring the 'dessert' behind the counter. "Or do you want something closer to the action?"

It wasn't lost on Peggy as to who was chosen to work where. Wasn't the first time no one noticed Peggy.

Roxie looked at their server's face and then to her name tag. "Peggy, we would love some chili and corn bread to go."

"How many alarms on the chili?"

"Uh, what?" Les was pulled out of his trance by the word 'alarm'.

Peggy knew this couple were first timers. She moved to block Les from watching Amanda.

"For the chili. One is for Mama's boy. Five is for the Criminally Insane."

Roxie said to Les, "Collins said mild, so we should do one."

To Peggy, "Let's stick with Mama's boy. It isn't for us. I would like your meat loaf and a lemonade."

"Honey, you didn't even see our menu. How did you know we had meatloaf?" Peggy asked curiously.

Roxie smiled at Peggy. "This is a diner. Diners always have some classic like meatloaf."

For the first time in this century, Peggy smiled. "I like you, Sugar. You're not from around here. Deep South, maybe? Lower Louisiana?"

Roxie changing to her native accent, "Oui, Sha. Outside Nawlins. How you know dat?"

"Comes with the territory. You spend your life on a ribbon like the I-70, you eventually run across everything here. How about you?" Looking at Les.

"You have a classic burger?" he asked.

"How about a meatloaf burger?"

"Uh okay, and some onion rings and a Dr. Pepper."

"Traveling through? Honeymoon?" Peggy asked.

Roxie showed her badge. "Neither. We are here to see your famous attraction." Eyeing Amanda. "FBI."

Peggy lost her smile, probably for another century. "What's she done now that the FBI have to be called in?"

"We just need to talk to her."

"I'll call her over and get your order going. Just don't piss her off. We don't need no more incidents. Verl won't be pleased."

Peggy walked away and went behind the counter to confront Amanda. Whatever she said, Amanda looked over toward the agents sitting at the booth with unpleasant surprise. The truckers who were entertained by Amanda also turned to Roxie and Les. Amanda got a towel, wiped her hands, and left the counter. As she approached, Les moved out of the booth and sat next to Roxie. He motioned for Amanda to sit across from them.

"Sorry I'm working. What do you need?" she said, annoyed at losing her audience.

"Agent Cormier," Roxie said showing Amanda her badge. "This is Agent Michaels. FBI."

"So?" Amanda started to get up out of the booth.

"Please sit down," Roxie said. "This is not a social call."

"Good to know, because my dance card is filled up. So why are you here?" asked Amanda, "Is this about the asshat trucker and chili in his face? Was he some kind of special agent like you two?"

Roxie got right to the point. "Do you know a Bobbie Lee Johnson?"

"Should I?"

Les pitched in. "How about Jennifer Bishop, Pei Leung, Ginger Tervil, Indira Patel, Carol Meyers?"

"Those are names from long ago." Amanda said, looking out the window. Her annoyance had been replaced some pensive feeling.

Les continued, "Wendy Stern, Annie Rhodes, Stacy Kaplan?"

"More names from the past."

"Six of them are dead," Roxie said. "Murdered. Shall we continue?"

"Damn." Amanda said, surprised. "Who killed them?"

"How did you know these women, and why do you think we are here?"

"Well, I certainly didn't kill them. You think I did it?"

"Amanda, how were you connected with these women?"

Amanda explained, "We were the Nine Dotties, a group we formed at a Math Camp a few years ago. Damn. Who's left?"

Les added, "You, Patel, and Meyers."

"Amanda, do you know Bobbie Lee Johnson?"

Amanda sat there staring out the window. Roxie and Les let her process her memory. Then they saw Amanda get uneasy and squirm in her seat.

"That little turd. That little OCD mama's boy."

"Who are you talking about?" Roxie interrupted.

"The know-it-all Bobbie Lee. So quiet, So unassuming, so shy."

"Bobbie Lee Johnson?"

"Yeah. He was in another group, but he kept hanging around us. Indie, uh Indira seemed to capture his attention. He would hover near us, but never come over and talk to her."

"So, what did he do to you that you have such dislike for him?"

"It was just a prank that went horribly wrong."

"Ms. Horsch."

"Manda. As you can see by my surroundings, I don't rate a title."

"Okay, Manda. What did he do to you and your friends?"

"Damn. It's not what he did to us, it's what we did to him. Damn."

Amanda started fidgeting in her seat. It was not supposed to have gone this far.

"A little too much trash talk," Les said. "Can you trash talk with math?"

"Wish it were just math. We kind of led him on a little. Nine Sirens beckoning him on the rocks of destruction."

"So, Bobbie Lee was this shy math kid, and you girls seduced him?"

"Seduced? Hell no, but we were just playing with him. One day we were sitting together, and Bobbie Lee came up to us. I guess he finally got the nerve to talk to Indie. He was just standing there trying to say something. Damn!"

"And you started teasing him, all nine of you?"

"Well I had it with the little stalker, so I thought I would end his little charade. I came up next to him and started acting as if I was trying to make out with him. Since I was the least shy of the others and had a nicer rack than Indie, I figured a little attention from Manda would scare him away."

"And did your feminine wiles do the trick?" asked Les.

"Probably a little more than planned. Kid got so turned on that he popped. It became obvious to the others what happened. Consequently, we all started laughing. The kid turned beet red and ran with his boy juice soaking his pants for all to see."

"Incroyable," said Roxie, as she pondered Amanda's use of the word "popped". She only knew that word was used by porn stars and hoped that Amanda had not gone that route.

"Louisiana French?"

"Yes, how did you know?"

"Interstate? Truck stop? Truckers from all corners of the U.S.? I see and hear it all."

"What happened after his unfortunate experience with you and your friends?" asked Les.

"The plan worked. We never saw him again. Mommy probably came down and picked him up early. I can't imagine the conversation between those two when he got home having to explain the soiled laundry."

"Did you ever see his mother? Perhaps when she dropped him off?"

"Nah, but I heard things."

"Like?"

"Kid was seriously OCD or anal retentive, whatever. Everything had to be ordered, arranged, labeled. Bobbie Lee, I heard, was a brilliant mathematician, but he had no social skills. Some say it was his mother."

"Overprotective?"

"Probably. I'm sure she whipped his ass into the next time zone once she got him home and discovered her future grandchildren were drying in his tighty whities. Worse yet. Wouldn't surprise me, if she was upset that his juices were wasted on some girl his age and not her."

"Oedipus Complex?"

"Man, who knows? More like Joan Crawford and wire hangers. You want your killer? Find Bobbie Lee."

"He'll be coming after you."

Amanda wriggled more in her seat. She looked uncomfortable.

"Don't care," she said. "Could be something to look forward to just to shake up my awesomely miserable life."

"Manda. It seems as if you had everything. Looks. Brains. Might I ask what happened?" asked Les.

"Don't matter. After high school, I went to Oklahoma State. Partied, Got roofied and raped. Woke up in a park naked. Painted like a canvas: 'Slut whore do me for a good time'. That was enough for me. I checked out. Drifted. The wind blew me here. I don't know how you found me, but Bobbie Lee will never find me. I'm off the radar, off the grid. Not even Google Maps will find me."

"You said Bobbie Lee was brilliant. He may have enough smarts to track you down," said Roxie. "Is there some place you can go for a little while, until we catch him?"

"Just because of our prank? You don't know that he is the one who killed these people. Hell, he is probably still nursing on his mother's lap for all we know."

"Manda, do you have any other info on this Bobbie Lee?"

"I never knew where he came from."

"You recognized my accent. Did Bobbie Lee have one?"

Amanda pondered the notion for a moment.

"As a matter of fact, yes he did," Amanda said. "The only thing about this job that means anything to me, catching peoples' accents and then finding out where they're from. Minnesota, northern Midwest, maybe. Sometimes when he did speak, it was almost as if you were watching "Fargo". Just a hint of that Americanized Scandinavian sound."

"Any other piece of info you can remember about him?"

"Always had his iPod connected to his ears. Walked past me once in his own world. Volume was up real high, thought his eardrums were going to burst. It was probably his way of blocking out the world."

"Could you hear what was playing?" Les asked.

"Sounded like blues, I remember now. It seemed out of place for this kid. White boy, math nerd getting down on Johnny Lee Hooker, BB King, Eric Clapton."

"Yeah, it is out of place."

"I would say he probably had a black wet nurse, but I doubt his mother would let her precious boy share a tit with anyone else."

"Manda, thank you. You've been a great help. I can't tell you what to do, but disappearing even deeper than you are, might be a good idea for a while."

"Nah, I'm good. If anything, call me if you get him."

Amanda got up and walked back to her groupies. She turned on her smile as if nothing ever happened.

"Sounds like a revenge killing for sure," Roxie said to Les. "Boy gets embarrassed big time by a bunch of girls. He retaliates by leaving his mark on them. No sexual contact, because it wasn't about sex, it was about humiliation. Leaving his sperm on them was his returning the humiliation."

"Stomping on their throats was his way of saying 'you won't laugh at me anymore'." Les added.

"We have the list of camp attendees," said Roxie, reading through the list. "There is a Robert L. Johnson here. You don't suppose—"

"Way too coincidental. Robert Johnson. Bobbie Lee Johnson. Listens to Blues."

"White boy, math nerd. From the northern Midwest."

"Leaves his victims at an intersection."

"No. Crossroads." Roxie said, worried. "Robert Johnson apparently went to the crossroads to sell his soul to the devil. Looks like Bobbie Lee has done the same thing."

Peggy came back with Roxie and Les' meals. "Pay at the cashier when you're done."

The food was impeccable for being a diner. Roxie and Les savored every bit of it. They were not looking forward to the trip back to Denver or the next few days.

Would they be able to stop this Bobbie Lee from hurting anyone else? Was Carol Meyers his next victim? They doubted he would drive to Idaho for Indira Patel and drag her all the way to Louisiana.

As Roxie and Les got up to pay at the register, Amanda stopped her stage act and walked over to deal with the bill. "He is serious, isn't he?" Amanda asked.

"As serious as your five-alarm chili, Amanda," said Les. Amanda turned from her "je ne sais quoi" attitude to worried.

"I have a sister in Portland. Maybe I could visit her for a few days. That nerd won't ever find me there."

"Make it a week. Verl can handle your absence for that long. So will your audience," Les said.

"My audience is all I have anymore."

"You're a lovely woman, Manda, and intelligent," added Roxie. "You have a lot more than your audience."

"Okay, Dr. Phil," said Amanda, cupping her breasts. "The girls have been good to me. I don't know if my brain has much to offer me anymore. They are all I have. They get me places."

Les was mesmerized by "the girls". But Roxie halted the show by handing Amanda her a card.

"Here is my number. Call me in one week."

"Sure, whatever. Food is on me, Agents."

"That's nice of you, Amanda. Take care of yourself," said Les handing her the check and a fifty.

Amanda said nothing. She put the check in her pocket and the fifty in her bra and walked away.

Roxie smiled and said to Les. "Free dinner and a show, huh?"

"Perks of our jobs, Agent Cormier."

"Or is that perkiness?"

Les said nothing as they walked out of the diner and headed back to Denver. The almost two-hour drive was boring, and the smells of chili and corn bread were making the trip unbearable.

"So, what's our next move?" Les asked.

"Drop this chili and corn bread off to Chief Collins."

"I mean after that?"

"Get some rest and get a flight home, then look for Carol Meyers."

"Then Louisiana?"

Roxie didn't answer. She just stared off into the Colorado flatness.

"Everything okay? You're excited to get back to Cajun country, aren't you?"

"Difficult memories, Les."

"Did you see on the map where this kid is going?"

"Yeah, so?" Roxie went into her accent. A place she goes outside herself when something bothers her. "He's going someplace that he probably never saw, a place that his math brain ain't helping him, the little peeshwank. The bayou don't like outsiders."

"You mean the people of the bayou."

"No, Sir. The bayou ain't happy. It's God's special place, for peace-lovin' people, strong people who want the world to stay away. Ain't endin' well."

Roxie sensed something was not right about their conversation with Amanda. She seemed too la-di-dah about the possibility of being a victim, and it bugged her all the way back to Denver.

Chapter Thirty-Six - Indira Gamal

After the long trip to Wisconsin, then to Colorado and back home, Roxie was exhausted. Her mind was trying to figure out what to do. Normally, she was more able to react to an immediate problem and deal with the issues as they poured out to her.

This problem was different. It was Saturday. She could go to the store, get her hair and nails done. Fix up her place. Anything. Because she had time. She figured Bobbie Lee was not going to kill anyone until Wednesday. She would have the whole weekend if she wanted it.

But like any good agent, she couldn't let it go. Her hair and nails had to take back seat. Bobbie Lee had his sights on his victim. It was a small group of women. The Nine Dotties. There were only three left. Indira Patel seemed too far away, and according to Amanda Horsch, it seemed as if Bobbie Lee liked Indira.

But the minds of killers don't function like the rest of humanity. Plus, he needed to finish his game. Complete the puzzle of the nine dots. His anal-retentive behavior was driving him. There had to be three more victims. Roxie needed some assurances.

Roxie rolled out of bed. A meager shower and breakfast later, she went into the office. On her desk were the contact numbers for the remaining two women from

Math Camp's Nine Dotties. Each time she saw the name of that group, it made her skin crawl.

She dialed Indira Patel's number. It was seven in the morning in Idaho on a Saturday. Indira should be home. The phone rang a few times, and someone picked it up. The voice sounded like the person had been sleeping. It was a woman's voice.

"Seven on a Saturday morning, this better be good."

"Good morning, I'm sorry to bother you, but—"

"I'm sorry to pick up the phone," Indira interrupted. "No, I don't want my business to have any more of your benefits."

"Wait, this is not a robo call. This is Agent Cormier of the FBI," Roxie said hoping that Indira would not hang up.

"Oh, that's a new ploy. What do you want, Agent Cormier from the FBI?"

"Is this Indira Patel?"

"Indira Gamal, Patel is my maiden name."

"I'm sorry to interrupt, but I need to ask you some questions."

"It can't wait until at least maybe 7:30?"

"I can call back if you—"

"No, sorry. I had a rough night. Can I wake up first and call you back in a little bit?"

Roxie gave Indira the number and hung up. She pondered Albert Einstein's thought experiments about the Theory of Relativity. If you put a boy on a swing next to a pretty girl, an hour would seem like only a minute. If you took the same boy and put him on a hot stove, a minute would seem like an hour. Waiting for someone to return a call was like sitting on the stove, not the swing. When you don't want it to, time stands still.

Roxie thought about what Indira was doing, probably got up, went to the bathroom, washed her face, looked at her long dark hair in the mirror to make sure it looked nice for a phone call. Of course, Roxie was assuming that Indira had long dark hair and hoped she would never have to meet her. The phone finally rang. "Cormier."

"This is Indira Gamal. You called earlier? What does the FBI want with me? I am a citizen of the United States."

"Once again, I apologize for the early morning call, but this has nothing to do with checking up on you. I assure you."

"Well, that's a relief."

"Indira, do you remember Math Camp and the Nine Dotties? You were in that group."

"That's a long time ago. Yes, I remember."

"Have you had any contact with any of the other women in that group?"

"Not much. I mean we kept in touch on social media, but then life took us all in different directions, and we just lost contact. Why? What happened?"

"I'm sorry to say that six of the Dotties have been murdered and we are trying to save the last three. You are one of them."

"Oh no."

There was a long pause on the line.

"Indira. Are you okay?"

Roxie could hear weeping.

"Who did this?" Indira asked.

"Do you remember Robert Johnson? Went by Bobbie Lee?"

"You think he did this?"

"We have reason to believe so, yes."

"I knew their prank would backfire on them."

"You mean the other girls teasing him into an embarrassing situation?"

"You know about it. Who told you?"

"Amanda Horsch."

"So, she wasn't his first victim. She should have been. After that incident, I called her 'Amanda Whore'. She went too far with her body. Now look where it got her."

"Apparently Bobbie Lee liked you."

"Yeah. And I liked him. He had an incredible mind. It was exhilarating to talk to him. I guess that's how the whole thing got started. He just picked the wrong time to talk with me. I tried to tell the other girls not to do that to him, but they had to finish. To embarrass him so badly he would never come around them again. I didn't expect him to go this far."

"Has he had any contact with you at all?"

"No. After the incident, I never saw him again. And I was too ashamed to get in touch with him. You said three were left. Who was the other one?"

"Carol Meyers."

"How did they die? Wait. I don't want to know. Is Carol safe?"

"For all we know, she is. We just can't seem to locate her. Almost like she just fell off the face of the earth. Did she have a boyfriend?"

Indira started laughing.
"Boyfriend? Carol Meyers had no interest in boys. She preferred the female persuasion. A benefit of being with the Nine Dotties. She got off being with the rest of us. Even though the rest of us were straight, well I guess the rest were. She helped Amanda take Bobbie Lee out, you might say."

"Indira, do you have some place you can go for the next few weeks, at least?"

"Geez, Why so long?"

"We believe that is when Bobbie Lee will strike next. On Wednesday, the seventh."

"Wednesday's child is full of woe."

"You knew his birthday?"

"Yes. I was in charge of birthdays for everyone at Math Camp, in case one of us had one during that time."

"Well, I need to make sure you're safe, and then I can focus on Carol Meyers."

"Thank you. And yes, I can go visit my mother in San Diego for a few days."

"That would be great, and can you please call me on the eighth, so I know you're okay?"

"I can do that. Good luck to you, and if you can get to Carol, tell her I said hello."

"That would make my day for sure."

Chapter Thirty-Seven – El Paso

Roxie concluded the conversation with Indira. Les had walked into the office. She was getting ready to greet him when her phone rang again.

"Cormier."

"Agent Cormier?" the voice said on the other side. "This is Officer Reynaldo, El Paso PD."

"How may I help you?"

"Responding to the BOLO you put out on a Bobbie Lee Johnson."

"Putting you on speaker. What do you have?"

"We have the blue Sonata. One of our officers spotted a car matching the description. Made a routine traffic stop."

"Was Bobbie Lee driving?"

"No. The driver and his passengers said they had purchased the car legally on Craigslist. They had the title signed and everything. With a bill of sale."

"Merde. Did they say anything about the seller?"

"The officer who stopped them said it was some white guy. He thinks the new owners were going to do one of those Craigslist robberies where they take your money and your car. Only thing they said was the car was in perfect condition, not a scratch. Impeccably clean. When asked how much, the guy said 3000. They laughed and said 300. There was no argument. A deal like that there would have been no reason to rob the guy."

"How long ago was this?"

"Bill of sale was dated December of last year. Everything looked legit. Only problem was the pendejos didn't bother getting a new license plate. They were driving around in a car with a Wisconsin plate. It looked a little suspicious. They didn't seem to have enough sense among them to fill a taco."

"Did you do a search in the car?"

"Yes, they were quite cooperative seeing that they forgot the license thing."

"Find anything?"

"There was a CD of John Lee Hooker under the driver seat. They said it wasn't theirs."

"I guess Blues was not on these gentlemen's playlists."

"No, Agent Cormier. Can't imagine that. We found nothing else. We had to let them go. Everything else seemed above board. We gave them a citation about the plate. But we did run the VIN. The owner was a Bobbie Lee Johnson."

"Did these guys say where the exchange was made?"

"Let me see," Reynaldo said, shuffling papers. "Walmart parking lot, north side."

"Officer Reynaldo. is there any way that you can check for any murders or suspicious deaths in that area within a few days of December 7, 2016?"

"Sure, be glad to. Something specific?"

"Add an Elbert Fillmore to the search, if you please."

"Call you back at this number?"

"Yes, I'll be here."

Roxie and Reynaldo hung up.

"What is Johnson doing in El Paso?" asked Les.

"He's not there to sample border cuisine. It only means one thing."

Roxie's phone rang again. "Cormier."

"Reynaldo here. Hey, we did a check for homicides during the period you asked. White male, middle 40's. But it has a DEA flag on it. I can't give you any further info. You will have to contact them."

"We'll check it out. Thanks," Roxie said as she hung up.

"Any reason our boy is into drugs?" she asked Les.

"Hell, not from his profile, but you never know. Call DEA and talk to them," Les said.

Chapter Thirty-Eight - DEA

Roxie got on the phone to DEA, an Agent Alvarez.

"Agent Alvarez, Roxie Cormier from the FBI, St Louis office."

"Agent Cormier. Nice to meet you," said Alvarez. "What does your office want with the DEA?"

"Elbert Fillmore. His name was flagged by your office. He might be a victim in a serial murder along with young women we are working on."

Roxie could hear papers shuffling through the phone.

"Agent Cormier, we don't know if this is a gang murder or not," said Alvarez, reading some documents. "If you think your cases are connected, they don't seem to be. Yours are women. This is some middle-aged man. He was found dead in north El Paso. His genitals were removed from his body."

"That's Bobbie Lee's father. I do appreciate you filling in the details, but is there any way you can prove it is not gang related?"

Alvarez pondered for a moment.

"I have a CI. He has a pulse on gang stuff. Let me see if I can get anything from him."

"Great. Call us back."

"Yeah, I have to go make a stop beforehand, but I will call you."

Agent Alvarez had the unpleasant task of finding Chuy Romero, gang member and Confidential Informant. Alvarez used him on a number of occasions, to be a watcher of illegal contraband crossing the border into El Paso.

Chuy was in a delicate situation as a Confidential Informant for the DEA. He had a family, including his Abuela, who took care of him when his parents dropped him off with a coyote promising the Romero family the dream of America. Instead, they got a son who was recruited young by MS 13. Chuy made a deal with his "Jefes". He would do anything for them, but Abuela was off limits. Jefe agreed, but Chuy knew promises were shallow. Chuy delivered, and Abuela was safe.

When Agent Alvarez caught Chuy in a sting operation smuggling cocaine, Alvarez gave him a chance. He was only fourteen, and Alvarez knew about the Abuela pact and used it against young Chuy. The kid had no choice but to comply.

Four years later, Alvarez went to Chuy Romero's place, outside the prying eyes of the good and bad worlds in which Chuy lived. Single level adobe house, chain link fence, bars on the windows, kitty litter landscape, and a black jockey statue in the front yard. Alvarez marveled about the statue. It didn't fit the west Texas xeriscape of this rundown part of El Paso. Alvarez knocked on the door. Chuy Romero answered.

"Another shakedown, huh, Vato?"

"Chuy my man, you're not happy to see me?"

"Oye, cabron. You smell of popo. You know I ain't dancing salsa with the Trece."

"Senor Chuy. This is another matter."

"I thought she was eighteen, man."

Alvarez laughed.

"You wish."

"Then what you bringing your sorry burro here for then? Especially with Abuela here."

From the back room, the voice of an older woman was yelling out something in Spanish.

"Calma te, Abuela. Un amigo visita."

"Wow. When did I become your amigo, Chuy?"

"You ain't. Just keeping Abuela from being spooked. Did you bring it? The payment?"

"A deal is a deal, amigo."

Alvarez held up a large burlap bag when he came to the door. He knew that too many people have eyes. And flashing dead presidents around that part of town was a bad idea. Instead, Alvarez brought something more precious than money.

"Twenty pounds Hatch Green."

"Non-roasted."

"As always."

Alvarez handed the bag to Chuy. To him, a bag of green chiles for his Abuela would make Chuy sing for anything. Chuy didn't need to be flaunting money around. People would notice. But green currency of the chile kind was something the two would agree on.

"More than the usual amount, Vato. Must be a big request, no?"

"I need some professional advice."

"Man, I'm staying away from the Trece. You know that."

"This may not be about the 13."

"Well, screw you, if you think I'm giving you Abuela's green chile stew recipe."

"Damn, on pain of death, no way."

"Then what're you dragging your ass out here for?"

"You heard about the guy up north, found without his jewels."

"It got around. Something like that causes a buzz in the lines."

"Sound gang-related to you? Maybe rival gangs?"

"The vic, as you popos call it, was a white guy. Ain't no rival stuff. Besides they whacked off his pene. That ain't a gang M.O."

"Why not?"

"Man, don't you read? You mess with the gangs around here you lose your big head, not your little head. There is some respect. We don't go chopping off some guy's churro. Vato, go back to Gang 101."

"Any talk of who may have done it?"

"Abuela watches Dr. Phil. She knows more than you. This was a revenge killing, maybe a lover, some puta, or even puto, depending on the way he swings it. Well, he ain't swinging anything anymore." Chuy started to laugh.

"So, this was a crime of passion."

"You asked my advice. You paid. I answered. Vete."

"Give Abuela my love, and thanks."

Chuy didn't reply. He just closed the door. Abuela got the chiles, Alvarez got his answer.
When Alvarez got back to his office, he contacted Agent Cormier. Roxie picked up when he called.

"Cormier," Roxie said. "Any word on our victim?"

"My CI heard about the murder. Said it was not gang related. More of a revenge killing. A killing by someone who didn't want his Johnson having any more action, if you know what I mean."

"Fortunately, I do. We put out a BOLO on a Bobbie Lee Johnson earlier. We think the two may have been related."

"Names don't match, could be Bobbie Lee's father from Fillmore's birth records. Sounds like sonny didn't want any more brothers or sisters. What about the Mrs. Johnson?"

"Found dead. Possibly murdered by the son also."

"Chutzpah."

"Not your average Spanglish, Agent Alvarez."

"Not your average parental love. I didn't get any BOLOS on my end, but if a name like this pops up on our radar, you will get a call from my office."

"Excellent, because we believe this kid is not done killing."

"Damn. Should our locals be involved?"

"At this time, no. We think he is headed east, maybe into Louisiana."

"Good riddance. He ain't welcome here, but just in case."

"We will let you know."

Chapter Thirty-Nine – Position Nine

The calendar was fast approaching Wednesday June 7. There were still no leads on Carol Meyers. Roxie was poring over the names and information she had collected from Khalid's secretary, when her phone rang.

"Cormier."

"Agent Cormier, this is Officer Rivers from the Edina, Minnesota Police Department."

"Officers Rivers, how may I help you?"

"I think we found a car matching the BOLO you put out on an Elbert Fillmore and Bobbie Lee Johnson."

"Yes, exactly. What do you have?"

"The car was found abandoned in the parking lot of an office building in Edina."

"What's your connection?"

"It seems as if a woman named Carol Marsh was reported missing by her boss. She didn't come in this morning. She worked at SportsStats, the office where we found the abandoned car. Her car is gone."

"Did you contact her?"

"We got the number from her boss and called it. Some guy answered. We figured it was her boyfriend. He hung up."

"I need you to have an officer go to her place and verify that she is there. Ms. Marsh does not have a boyfriend. She prefers women."

"As you wish. I will get right on it." Rivers hung up.

Officer Lois Sanders received the call to have a face-to-face verification of Carol Marsh. Sanders knocked on the door of the apartment. There was no answer, no activity. The officer knocked again, this time a little harder, when the door next to Marsh flew open.

"Damn, don't you see she ain't in. Oh crap, the police."

An elderly black woman was standing at the doorway in her morning muumuu.

"This is a welfare check for Carol Marsh, sorry for the loud banging."

"Hell, she got women goin' in and outta here all the time and finally one night, they's peace and quiet. Ain't nobody in there."

"We have reason to believe that she may have been with her boyfriend yesterday."

The woman laughed so hard that Officer Sanders was worried the lady's wig would come flying off.

"Oh child, someone need to get they facts straight. Carol dear is a lezzie. Ain't no one gonna have a chance with her, unless they has the same plumbing. Hell, she never came home after she went to work yesterday. Figured she be doin' the nasty with other lezzies. You feel me?"

"Yes, ma'am," Sanders said and handed her a card. "She comes back you give me a ring, okay?"

"I think about it. Have a nice day, Miss Officer."

When Officer Sanders got back to the patrol car, she called in the report, which was routed to Agent Cormier.

Les got on his phone to Edina. "I need an APB on a Carol Marsh. We need DMV to give us make, model and license number of her car. And a photo id from her driver license. Have SportsStats check their security cameras for the weekend and this morning and see if they have a visual on that part of the parking lot."

Edina police promised a quick response.

"He's taken her hostage, and has switched to her car," Roxie said.

"Can we be sure that she is still alive?"

"Bobbie Lee has to finish his game. He can't kill her now. Wednesday is in two days, and he couldn't stand the smell if she started decaying. Even in Minnesota, you know."

The phone rang.

"Michaels."

"Edina office calling. We have the info you requested on Carol Marsh. She drives a 2014 red Jeep Grand Cherokee."

"Great news. Thanks." Les hung up.

"We need to call off the APB for Carol and stop any police authority from picking up a 2004 Jeep with the wrong license plates between Minnesota and New Orleans," said Roxie.

"A risky move, Roxie," Les said. "Are you sure you wanted to do that?"

"If the kid gets spooked, he may finish her prematurely."

"Like I said, risky. I'll cancel the APB and put a word out to State Highway patrols along the way, just to watch for the vehicle and call any reports in."

"That works for me. I hope it works for Ms. Marsh."

"How did we miss the difference in names? Marsh and Meyers aren't even close. Couldn't have been that big a mistake."

"Let me call Indira Patel and see if she knows anything."

Chapter Forty – Social Media

Roxie got on her phone and placed a call to Indira.

"Agent Cormier, what a surprise to hear from you so quickly," Indira answered.

"Sorry to bother, but we have no records on a Carol Meyers anywhere."

"Well, that is odd, since you are the FBI."

"But we do have a Carol Marsh. Does the name sound familiar?"

"No."

"You said you had been in contact with the Nine Dotties on social media?"

"Yes, Facebook. But I had not been on for a long time. What's the problem?"

"What is the group name you used?"

"Just go to my profile and do a Friend Request. The links should all be there. I am still under my maiden name: Patel."

Roxie thanked Indira, hung up, and logged into her desktop. She didn't want to use her personal profile, so she created a new account. BayouSnakeGirl sounded cool.

She found Indira's profile and made a Friend Request. Indira must have been waiting on the other end, because the request was approved in a matter of seconds.

Time to do some surfing, she thought. Roxie went through all of Indira's Friends and Friends of Friends. There were hundreds. Indira was telling the truth about not being on much. Her last posting was over a year ago.

Sadly, she found some of the other Nine Dotties. A few had memorials posted expressing love to the departed, offers of rewards to anyone who knew the killer or killers.

Roxie found Carol Meyers under Stacy Eddings' friends. If only she had gotten to Stacy in time.

"Les, come over here," Roxie said.

Les walked up behind Roxie and noticed she was on Facebook. "Personal time catching up with all your BFFs?" he asked.

"Carol Meyers. Look," she replied.

"Damn. How did you get that?"

"Indira."

"Look at her postings."

"Hmm. Only two words on the last one: Damn Lover. I bet a beignet that Carol Meyers got screwed by an ex, took her money or her love, and ruined her, maybe stalked her."

"Then she goes through the process of getting a new identity. Didn't want to get new monogrammed towels, so she changed it to Marsh."

"Now we have the connection. I am sure we can get a search of legal name changes."

"So, what's your plan now?"

"We're headed to New Orleans, but first I have to make a call."

"To whom?"

"A good buddy of yours."

Chapter Forty-One ~ The Call

Roxie picked up her phone and dialed south.

"Moyes Swamp Tours. Moyes speaking."

"Linc? Assemble the boys. Ten am sharp. Your place."

"Nuff said."

Lincoln Moyes hung up the phone. He got a worried look on his face. Few people called him Linc. It was reserved for those who showed him the utmost respect. It was also a name that put fear in his eyes.

It happened one time when some large white punk came on a swamp tour with some of his buddies. They were drinking and causing a ruckus with the other guests.

They made the unfortunate mistake of trying to mess with a white girl half this troublemaker's size. Little did they know, she was an FBI agent skilled in martial arts, who was in the bayou with troubled kids showing them a harsher life than they had at home.

"Hey sexy, wanna have a good time with me and the guys?" white guy said.

A lack of response and a show of disinterest by walking away, got Dumbo mad. He grabbed her by the shoulder. Mistake.

The bully woke up later in St Ann's Hospital: two broken ribs, a broken collar bone, and a bad headache. He was also wearing a pair of shiny handcuffs.

Moyes didn't fear the bayou, but he feared little Roxie. She earned his respect and was allowed to call him Linc.

"But only in case of emergencies" she said.

"I don't have any buddies named Linc," Les said.

"Lincoln Moyes, Les. Your large and frightening buddy."

"Oh, him."

"But you must call him, Mr. Moyes."

"Not a problem."

"We need to go to New Orleans. Bring plenty of clothing. Long sleeve shirts. Muck boots."

"Yeah, yeah. I have been there."

"If I remember you were wearing Cole Hahns last time. You can leave those home."

Chapter Forty-Two – The Meeting

Little was said to gather the gentry of the bayous together. Once Moyes was off the phone with Roxie, the call went out on the CB and HAM channels. The message was terse. "Roxie needs a gathering. Ten sharp."

Everyone on the water respected Moyes. Everyone on the water feared Roxie, after the Dumbo incident. They all knew that if Moyes called, offering assistance to their favorite FBI agent, this was serious. Someone was getting the cunja.

Moyes closed the tours in the morning, stating some kind of outbreak, and to come back tomorrow. Those who had come all this way to ride a tour boat were not happy. It only took Moyes, large black Moyes, to step out and say gently, "We closed. Come back. You get a discount."

Moyes didn't explain what the discount was. Maybe it was 50% less mosquitos.

Roxie and Les pulled in about five minutes before ten. There was no murmuring as to what the emergency was all about. As the agents walked in, all heads turned to the door, and silence fell.

"Mr. Moyes. Thank you for calling this impromptu meeting," Roxie began.

Moyes just nodded at Roxie and gave the evil eye to Les. Good thing Les got smart from his previous visit to Moyes swamp tours. He brought in a black satchel, set it up on the counter and unloaded 12 jars of the finest gold you can get in this area. The evil eye was replaced by a wry smile and a simple nod of acceptance.

"You can share it, Mr. Moyes."

"Much obliged, Agent." Moyes placed one jar of honey under the counter and motioned for his partner to pass the others around."

"Hoo wee. Now they some good stuff," Albert said, smiling. "Must be something big coming down, huh, Miss Roxie."

As any lady from the South would know, it doesn't matter the station in life, all men should be spoken to with respect, and the group here deserved it as much as any.

"Yes sir, Mr. Albert Bondurant. I hope Nellie and the kids they doing fine."

"Rightly so, yes, ma'am."

Roxie scanned the room acknowledging each man seated or standing there.

"Mr. Finney, Mr. Gaspard, the gentleman Sauvage, Pere Chastain, Mr. Franks. I want to thank all of you for taking your time to come to this gathering. We have a problem."

"Someone comin' to play hanky-panky in the backwater, Miss Roxie?" asked Franks.

"I'm layin' it straight out to you. We have a serial killer coming to do his deeds here."

Murmuring.

Roxie continued, "I don't want y'all to fret none. We do not believe your families are in danger. We think he has a hostage. A woman. The game he is playing has resulted in six deaths already. I don't want a seventh, not here."

"You couldn't stop him before he got here? Respectfully speaking."

"No, Mr. Sauvage, but we didn't want to spook him and possibly hurt this woman he is with."

"Bayou gonna spook him even more. Where this boy from?"

"Wisconsin."

Laughing among the group.

"Hell, Miss Roxie, that peckerwood is crazy, thinking he can come here and mess with the bayou. It'll chew him up and spit him out like a gator who ate too many tourists."

More laughing. Moyes hushed the group.

"What do you want from us, Miss Roxie?" Moyes asked.

"I need eyes. This is a big place. Lots of places to hide. I don't know how he will get around. I don't know if he is armed. But I can tell you, he has a brilliant mind. His brain will tell him what to do."

"His brain ain't gonna help him here, Miss Roxie, you know dat."

"I do, Mr. Franks. That I do. I'm expecting him to mess up, to make the wrong turn, and get confused, and this will be our chance."

"So, we are just going to go on with our lives while this killer is around?"

"I want it to seem like a normal day on the bayou. But you have every right to protect yourself and family and property. I am having Agent Michaels here pass around pictures of our boy and his hostage, a Carol Marsh."

"What be his name?" asked Chastain.

"His name is Robert Johnson, he may be going by Bobbie Lee, or maybe Elbert Fillmore, his father's name."

"Robert Johnson? That boy sell his soul to the devil, too?"

"He got some bad voodoo on his head with a name like that," said Sauvage.

"Yes, he is a disturbed kid, may have killed his parents plus these six women."

"Bayou may let him in, but he ain't comin' out."

"If you see him, get on the radio. I doubt he will have any communication. Call into the office here. All of us will assist one another. I can't do it all by myself, gentleman."

"Like any bad gator, we gonna set a trap?"

"What you got in mind, Mr. Gaspard?" Roxie asked.

"Well, do we know where he is headed?"

"Bayou south of Kraemer."

"Why so particular? Ain't Bayou Teche good enough?"

Laughing.

"He is playing this numbers game. Specific coordinates. North of Bayou Baton Pilon is his target."

"Damn, that boy crazy. That's near Lucius Lafitte's place. White boy stick out like a sore thumb, he will."

"Lucius ain't here. Up in Vicksburg for a funeral. Auntie Flora," said Boudin.

Everyone bowed their heads and took off their caps.

"May she rest in peace," said Bondurant.

"Ain't no peace here, if we got a killer coming," Boudin added.

"So, I'll take your ideas for a trap," Roxie said.

"Only way he getting down here is on 307. Maybe, all of a sudden, he see a pirogue on the bank by the road. Little bit of gas. Something to tease him."

"Excellent. But his victim might not be so willing to get in something small. We don't know how he has the woman restrained."

"We all just play it by ear. Life ain't changing for us here. Let him decide how he want to move."

"Remember, when you see him," Roxie warned. "Do nothing except report. You may be justified acting in your own defense, but I would like him alive."

"He can use my boat. Peeshwank betta give it back."

"The Mrs. won't be happy some cracker took her ride."

Laughter.

"Hell to pay. Ain't no backwater deep enough to hide from the Mrs., her transportation goes lost. Skin him and patch the holes in the roof."

More laughter.

"Seriously," said Roxie. "We have a dangerous mental case. He will be unpredictable. He will be on a mission and won't stop until he accomplishes the task."

"We do right by you, Miss Roxie and dat poor girl he carryin' down here."

"Looks like the weather will hold for us. This goes right we have a fais-do-do," said Sauvage smiling.

Les looked a little puzzled. Moyes noticed his confusion.

"Cajun for party, Agent Michaels, sheesh. You lucky you brought honey, else the boys strap yo ass to the front of Willie's airboat and see how many mosquitos you get stuck in yo pearly whites."

Roxie gave Moyes the look. "Mr. Moyes."

"Sorry, Miss Roxie," he said, penitent and moving back a few feet past the length of her arm."

"Now go about your business. Agent Michaels and I will be at Miss Douillard's place."

Moyes walked back behind the counter and brought out his prized jar of gold.

"No need, Mr. Moyes," Les said. "I held a few back."

"She like that."

"Any questions before we get back to our life?"

There were no questions, but these people were not getting back to their lives. Someone was coming to disrupt the life on the bayou. It was planned, and they were warned. Like a hurricane coming from the east, the people knew what to do. They also knew that the backwater would absorb the winds and rain. The backwater will absorb the killer, too.

Hell to pay.

Chapter Forty-Three – A Day Early

Bobbie Lee got off Interstate-10 and headed south. He was almost there. The coordinates he had entered into his GPS were showing an arrival in less than half an hour. Problem was, he was a day early. He didn't plan on Position 9 being so easy. He met her at her place of work in the parking lot.

Thanks to Facebook, he thought, for making people so accessible, especially stupid people who give out more information than they should.

Bobbie Lee thought about running some analytics proving a direct correlation between the size of one's profile to their vanity.

Carol was an easy target. She didn't recognize him right away. He pretended to be the poor lost soul, heavy on the Northern Plains accent.

"Where is the I-35 freeway?" he asked.

She unlocked the car door, and without so much as a kind word, just pointed, "Back on 35 North. You'll see the signs."

Carol saw nothing after that. She heard nothing but woke up a while later with a splitting headache in the back of her own car with a driver she knew even less. Until he introduced himself, of course.

Chapter Forty-Four - Hellhound

Bobbie Lee just passed through Memphis on Interstate 35 and turned on his MP3 player. Robert Johnson played "Hellhound on My Trail". He smiled at his plan. *No one can figure out my plan, and I have to keep moving.*

Little did he know, someone else was humming another Robert Johnson song "Cross Road Blues". Moyes whispered to himself. *Lord above, have mercy on Bobbie Lee.*

Amanda Horsch crossed into Idaho on I-84 on the way to her sister's place in Portland. The radio was set to scan, when Boz Scaggs popped up, singing "Hell to Pay". She stopped the scan to listen. *The devil isn't at the Pearly Gates, Boz.* Amanda said to the radio. The devil is in Louisiana. A smile came over her face, long enough to hit scan again.

Indira Gamal packed for her trip to her mother in San Diego. She had the Pandora Channel set on her TV. The Who were playing "Behind Blue Eyes". She caught the phrase about love being vengeance, and a chill ran through her.

Chapter Forty-Five ~ Old Memories

"Bobbie Lee?" Carol cried.

Bobbie Lee did not respond, so Carol just lay in the back of her car, listening to the rhythmic beat of the road.

After a while her crying stopped, and a familiar, painful scent came screaming at him from the back of the car. Bobbie Lee looked through his rear-view mirror to his contents in the back.

"Couldn't hold it in, huh? Another incontinent woman," he said disgusted.

She had wet her pants. After many hours on the road and being tied up, she had no choice but to relieve herself. One unpleasant situation down, a thousand to go.

After a moment of discomfort and silence from her captor, she began to show some anger. What could it hurt?

"Hey, take the damn ear plugs out of your ears, and listen to me," she screamed.

Bobbie Lee looked in the rear-view window. No one was behind him, so he slammed on the brakes. Carol was not belted in, and she crashed against the rear seats.

"Sonuvabitch," she screamed.

Another cut, more blood dripped from the side of her face.

Bobbie Lee stared at her through the mirror. "I'm listening."

"Look, I don't know what game you're playing, but I'm done."

"Sorry, Number Nine. It's not over until the fat lady sings."

Carol realized she was reduced to a number, a position in the Nine Dotties' stupid puzzle.

"I had no interest in Manda's little game she played with you," Carol said, upset and sore. "Hell, I wasn't interested in you at all, or in any geeky boy at camp."

"I know," he replied. "But you're just like all the rest."

"And you're not? Some snotty Momma's boy, who couldn't even keep in control. I bet you were a bed wetter. I'm lying here, pissed in my pants, and the smell brought back old memories, huh?"

Bobbie Lee floored the accelerator pedal and rocketed Carol hard against the back door. As he got back out on the road, he waited for a response. There was none. Carol was out. Just one too many knocks on the head. *They just don't know when to shut up*, he thought.

Chapter Forty-Six - Cholera

The air in the bayou was thick. But this time it wasn't the normal weather. Death was coming. Most of the time death comes as a surprise. This time it was planned. All was quiet, quieter than usual. Even the CB at Moyes Swamp Tours was quiet, not the usual backwater chatter. Words came over as cryptic, meaningless to the outsider.

"Teche like glass."

"Crickets are hushed."

"Marley's boat sank again."

This last comment raised a flurry of laughter. Maybe it was good to have some noise. Made it life as usual, perhaps. Maybe take the edge off. If Death was coming, it had better bring a smile. Honey would have been nice, but death ain't into cheery. The wait was unnerving Les.

Moyes was unnerved by Les as he paced back and forth.

"Slow down, Mr. G Man. Ain't these waters teach you nothing?"

"Like what, Mr. Moyes?" Les asked.

"Man, go slow like the water. City boy with all your traffic and schedules, timeline. Sheesh."

Roxie came into the lobby area where the command post was set up.

Moyes looked up at Roxie, needing some kind of familiar communication. "This boy armed?"

"Good question, Mr. Moyes."

Moyes was relieved she didn't say "Linc" in front of Agent Michaels.

"There was never a gun mentioned in any of the other murders. Let me get on the phone."

Moyes smiled. He enjoyed being a big help. Emphasis on big.

Roxie called El Paso. "Agent Alvarado. This is Agent Cormier. We spoke the other day."

"Oh, yes. Did you get your man?"

"Not yet, but can you please check to see if your records show any firearms registered to Elbert Fillmore?"

"Sure, let me get on it, and I will call you back."

Roxie hung up. Moyes sat back in his big chair, sipping a big soda, making the Cheshire Cat look like the Mona Lisa.

"Changes things if he carrying," said Moyes.

Roxie hoped that Bobbie Lee would stick to his M.O. and not add any more surprises.

Roxie's phone rang. She was listening. Les and Moyes were listening to her listening.

"Thanks, good news. What we expected." Roxie said as she hung up.

"Word?" Moyes asked.

"DNA from the mother was a parental match to the DNA in the semen found on our victims."

"We have our man," Les said clapping his hands.

"The tox screens also came back showing Shirley Johnson had Temazepam in her blood. She was taking it for insomnia," Roxie added.

Moyes watched the two agents exhilarated over the news. "Peckerwood out there in our backyard. You ain't got jack yet."

"Okay, we almost have our man," Les said.

Jesse came bounding into the lobby. "Linc, we got trouble. Some irate tourists want to know why they can't get a tour today. Web site says we open."

Moyes didn't move a muscle except what he needed to speak.

"Tell 'em we got cholera."

Jesse smiled, then started coughing.

"Yeah, sure." Cough, cough. "Sound good."

"Symptoms of cholera are nausea and diarrhea." Les said.

"I ain't faking that, no Sir," Jesse said shaking his head. "Go running out past them, screaming 'Cholera', holding your backside," Moyes said.

"They think I'm a damn fool."

Moyes just looked up at Jesse raising his eyebrows. Everyone broke up into a raucous laugh.

"For the good of the community, no?"

Moyes just nodded his head. Jess left and was heard moaning and groaning off in the distance.

Mr. Gaspard walked in, confused as hell. "What up with Jesse?"

"Cholera."

"Damn. Should we call Doc Ribeau?"

"Nope."

"Well, whatever he had, sure scared those tourists. They got in their rentals and headed outta town."

Moyes looked at Les who was sitting in a chair just shaking his head. "Life is simple here, Mr. G Man."

"Agent Michaels, Linc," Roxie said.

Moyes straightened up out of his slouch and looked down the barrel of those dark Acadian eyes and knew he was in trouble.

"Yes, ma'am. Sorry, Agent Michaels."

Roxie smiled and gave Moyes a big smile and a wink. The mountain was appeased, although she thought she heard "Cracker" come from his lips. Maybe she was mistaken, but the phone rang. It was agent Alvarado.

"What have you got for us, Alvarado?" she asked.

"Mr. Fillmore registered a Colt .45 and a Mossberg Over Under 12 gauge, but since we thought this was a DEA gang issue, we had done a complete inventory of the belongings in his house. The shotgun and pistol were not on the list."

"Hmm," Roxie pondered. "This is not good news. Thank you, Agent."

She hung up.

"Boy's carrying. Damn," Moyes said.

"Put out the word to the gents," Roxie advised.

Moyes walked over to the CB and picked up the mike.

"Breaker 24."

"Come on back," someone said on the other side of the airwave.

"Pillsbury is packing."

"Roger that."

A roll call of responses came floating in on the loudspeaker for a number of minutes.

"Pillsbury?" Les asked.

"White boy. We call him Pillsbury. Didn't you see Ghostbusters? All fluff."

"Got it," Les said, trying not to laugh too loud.

"But we gonna burn his ass."

Moyes was sure of it. It may not come down to "crossing the streams", but he was sure the bayou had a plan of its own. He wasn't worried.

Chapter Forty-Seven - Chackbay

A red Jeep Grand Cherokee drove silently through the river town of Gramercy, and on down to South Vacherie. It turned right onto 307 and headed for a small town called Chackbay.

Bobbie Lee's cargo was beginning to stir again. He needed to get to his destination quickly. He turned off to a road just north of Grand Bayou.

Bobbie Lee could see the boat from the road. It was a nice one, better than he expected. He remembered that he needed to thank his benefactor upon his next meeting.

He pulled the car to the back near the dock and hauled Number 9 to her awaiting watercraft. There was a note on the railing, saying the house was open if he needed it.

He was lucky that no one was around to see him or Number 9. Too lucky. Well, maybe not. Just to be safe, a tarp was waiting behind the house where he parked. After loading his game piece into the house, he went back and covered up the car.

"Breaker 24."

Everyone in the Swamp Tours lobby jumped.

"Showtime," Moyes said and returned an acknowledgment. "Come back."

"Breaker 24. This is Muttonchops. Snake Girl, you got your ears on?"

"Who the hell is Snake Girl?" Les asked.

Roxie grabbed the mike from Moyes.

"Snake Girl here. Nice to chat with ya, Mr. Chops."

"One red feather off 20."

"Damn," said Moyes. He landed too far west, the little peckerwood."

"Still got yer eyes on him, Chops?"

"That's a negatory. But I'm camped out here just off 20. He just disappeared."

"Okay. We're running silent. If Pillsbury is on the water, he may have ears."

"Let's go to the secondary channel."

"Um, breaker 24. This be Punch-Us Pilot."

"Come back."

"I seem to have forgotten the secondary channel."

"Damn," said Moyes. "Best laid plans of Mice and Men."

Moyes wanted it all to go so well in front of the agents.

"How many wives did Skinny McMurtrey have before he bought it?" Moyes asked.

"Roger that. Switching to secondary channel. Out."

Roxie looked over at Les, who just sat there as an audience in a play he never would have imagined.

"Five. Skinny had five wives," she said smiling but wanting to burst out laughing.

Moyes just shook his head. "Agent Michaels, what do you bring to this party?"

"Best darn sharpshooter in the St. Louis office," Roxie said. "Will ventilate a rat off the top of your head at 500 yards."

Moyes didn't like rats, and surely not one sitting on his head with Les on the trigger. He decided he would be nice to the FBI Agent from now on.

"Won't know what hit him," Les said.

"That's the plan," added Roxie.

When Bobbie Lee came inside the house, Carol was beginning to wake up. She was groggy and moaning, complaining about her pounding headache.

"If you behave yourself," he said to Carol, "I will untie you. You can have something to drink and rest."

"Why are you being so nice all of a sudden?" she asked. "Do what you have to and get it over with."

"Not time yet."

"What is this? Some ritual sacrifice that must take place during a full moon?"

"Just a game of nine dots. Besides, the moon will be full on the ninth, not the seventh."

"Only you would know that, Bobbie Lee."

She hated even saying his name, but if she could personalize him more, he would reciprocate and not consider her a number or a game piece.

"I need something for this headache."

Bobbie Lee untied the ropes.

"Get it yourself," he said.

A real gentleman, she thought. Now she knew why she preferred her own sex. Carol was too tired to run, too tired to scream, too sore to fight. It was just time to give in and see what all the fuss was about.

When she walked into the bathroom, she could smell herself. Shower time. Twenty minutes and all the hot water later, she walked out of the shower in just a towel. Bobbie Lee stared at her stunning body.

"I'm not putting on my dirty clothes," she said defiantly.

"Go find something. I don't want you walking around like that. Clothes or ropes. Your choice."

"Pansy ass momma's boy. You were so shy when Manda was all over you. I know why she seduced you. It was obvious."

Bobbie Lee was fed up. *Just can't get them to shut up*, he thought again. He wished the time would go by more quickly. It was a long way to the next position. He pulled out his father's Colt .45 and pointed it directly at Carol.

"Shut up."

Carol was not expecting the gun. Seeing the business end of the .45 scared her into silence. She didn't know he had it in him.

"The others were easy. They put up a fight and lost."

"What others?" Carol didn't know about the six victims before him, and of course, Bobbie Lee's parents.

"Pei, Annie, Ginger, Wendy, Stacy, Jennifer."

Carol sunk to the floor trembling. She started to cry.

"They're dead? How? You?"

It was time for Carol to use her brilliant mind and plan a way out.

"All a part of the game. And you're Number 9."

In spite of all the pounding in her skull, she managed to picture the three-by-three array of dots and where she was in the new arrangement. The bottom right. There were two left after her.

"Who's left?"

"Amanda and Indira."

Carol wondered why Amanda was not first. But she knew why. And she didn't figure that Indira would be a victim.

"You liked Indira. She liked you. Why kill her?"

"Because she didn't stop it."

Carol was mustering anger inside.

"You're an ass, Bobbie Lee. You had it all, you ass. Did you have this one-on-one fireside chat with the rest of your victims?"

"You better get some rest. Tomorrow is a special day."

Carol pondered the puzzle in her pounding head.

"Who are the outside points then? she asked.

"My mother and father."

Carol collapsed on the couch, shaking all over, not because she was almost completely naked and just out of the shower. But she realized that Bobby Lee was insane, and she was going to be next. Tears formed in her eyes.

"How could you?" she asked. "No, wait. I don't want to know."

"Better that you don't know. Now you need to get some rest. Tomorrow is a big day."

"Aww, our first date. What shall I wear?"

Carol didn't care anymore. She ripped off her towel, threw it at him and walked into one of the bedrooms. As soon as she hit the bed, she was out.

Bobbie was a light sleeper. He strategically placed himself in a chair in the hallway. Any sound from her, he would notice. She couldn't get out. He couldn't wait until tomorrow.

Before he crashed in the chair, he stood in the doorway where Carol slept. She lay flat on her stomach. Bobbie Lee liked her curves. He remembered the many times he watched his mother sleep. She never knew. It was his little secret.

If only Carol didn't hate men, he thought.

Bobbie Lee picked up the towel Carol had thrown and took it into the bathroom to hang it up. Her soiled clothes lay on the floor, reeking of urine. He used the towel to gather them and walked into the laundry room and dumped them in the washer.

I should have made her stand outside, he said to himself as he added detergent and started the wash.

Roxie sat outside by the boat dock watching the sun set through the thick forest to the west. She was thinking of all the victims, of Pei, her first case, of Carol. *Where was she? Was she safe? What had Bobbie Lee done to her?*

Les walked up to her. She was not startled by his presence. His boots made a distinctive sound.

"What do you want, Les? Any news?" she asked without turning around.

"I just came out to see how you were doing. And there has been no chatter at all since the first sighting."

"He's waiting for tomorrow. It'll be the seventh."

"How do you know he won't start after midnight?"

"You can see an almost full moon tonight, but these waters aren't good for night travel, even with a moon. He can't risk it."

"You're sure of his actions," said Les wanting to know what was dancing in her mind.

"It's a game, and he has to play it to the end. By the rules."

Chapter Forty-Eight - Revelation

Carol woke up with the sunlight blasting through the window. Every part of her was sore and bruised. It had been a while since she had a good night sleep, especially after these last few days. A sheet was draped over her that wasn't there when she fell on the bed last night.

The clothes she had ripped off in the bathroom were lying in a chair next to the bed, folded and neatly stacked. A fresh scent of honeysuckle emanated from them.

How kind of him, she thought. Perhaps she shouldn't hate men. There are some who may be redeemable. But then again, Bobbie Lee was going to kill her today. She decided she would continue to hate men.

Carol took her clothes to the bathroom and got dressed. Bobbie Lee had already been up. The chair in the hallway was gone and was returned to its original place. Looking around the house, Carol thought she could probably just walk right out the door, run down the street yelling that a mad man was going to kill her, and she would be saved any more pain and humiliation. Instead, she saw Bobbie Lee in the kitchen making breakfast.

"I hate to say this, but this whole scenario doesn't make sense to me. Whose place is this?" she asked.

"Good morning to you, too," he replied. "Friend of a friend. What's the problem?"

"Well, you washed my clothes, thank you. You didn't cut me up into little pieces as I lay sleeping in the bedroom, for which I am grateful. You're making breakfast, and it smells good. I don't get where we are going with this."

"You remind me of my mother," he said.

Crap, she thought. No woman wants to hear that from a guy. *I hope he doesn't ask me to nurse him.* Then she realized that he killed his own mother, and the fear of being captive again worried her.

"You killed your mother." She walked in to pick up some toast. "Guy kills his mother for only one reason. She either beat you, verbally abused you, all of the above, or you're just crazy. Is there jelly?"

"No, you remind me of her when I was very young."

Oh great. Now is when he is going to ask to be suckled.

"She was beautiful. She was loving, yet she was strong-willed."

"I'm not any of those, Bobbie Lee."

"I watched you last night sleeping."

Okay, now he is getting creepy.

"Every move of your naked body reminded me of her. You are beautiful."

"You watched your mother sleep naked? That's sick."

Carol would have enjoyed watching his mother, but not him. She did notice the jam was home-made by locals.

"Amanda was beautiful, too," she reminded him.

Carol knew it herself, personally.

"But you couldn't handle her seductions at camp."

Bobbie looked at her. She saw his cheeks flush. Was it embarrassment? Was it anger?

"It was new to me. I had never been with anyone before, and she came on too strong."

"You were a big boy. You could've stopped her before she even got started. But I think you liked it. Liked the attention. Liked the other girls watching. Maybe waiting for their turns?"

"No."

"Did mommy try the same thing? Single mom all alone, raising a handsome young man. Missing the intimacy of a husband, a lover?"

"Stop," Bobbie Lee said slamming down the butter knife on the counter.

"She did. Damn," she spoke toward Bobbie Lee, but she was actually speaking to herself aloud. "She seduced her own son. Incredible."

"No, she didn't. She didn't."

Bobbie Lee was taken back to a younger age, a time far in his past. He remembered Mother bathing him thoroughly. She dressed him, ensuring all his clothes fit well, as she ran her hands around him to make sure everything was well-placed.

"Well, I'll be, Bobbie Lee," she said in a rhythmic tone. "Your mother got to you before Amanda did. No wonder she had a hard time letting you go to camp."

"How did you know that?" Bobbie Lee asked.

He had never told anyone about his mother, let alone her reluctance to let him out of her sight. Carol was caught. She couldn't explain how she knew. So, her mind had to come up with a believable answer. A lie.

"Cathy Marx told me."

"My teacher?"

"Only Cathy Marx I know. She was at Math Camp with the rest of us. One of the chaperones."

Damn, that a was good lie.

Bobbie Lee knew why he could not trust a woman. Not only do they talk too much; they also talk too much with other women.

"It's time to go. I have something to complete."

This was Carol's last chance at saving herself. "I'm not going with you."

She was direct, matter of fact. Not trying to be contentious or getting herself shot. That was the way it was. Bobbie Lee pulled the .45 out of his waistband and pointed it at her. Carol was no longer afraid. In fact, she felt sorry for him, almost as if some motherly instinct in her kicked in and felt like he just needed someone to hold him and tell him it was okay.

"I need to finish the game," he said. His words spoke with a hint of fear and anger. "Games must come to an end. It's the rule."

"Murdering innocent women is not a game."

Bobbie Lee yelled at her. "They all made fun of me. They paid the price. Now, it's your turn."

"Sticks and stones. Grow up, Bobbie Lee."

Carol walked to the front door as Bobbie Lee pointed the gun at the floor and pulled the trigger. The bullet hit just a few feet from her. She stopped dead in her tracks. The noise was deafening in that small section of the house. She put her hands up to her ears. It didn't help that the headache she had from last night got compounded by the pressure wave of a bullet.

Carol began weighing her options. She was a sports statistician. She knew the odds of her getting out of this mess were not good. So, like anyone who deals with probabilities knows, if you can't change the odds, change the game. She raised her hands up.

"You win, Bobbie Lee."

He lowered the gun. "Time to go."

"Just don't go pointing that damn thing at me anymore," Carol said. She was no longer afraid, just pissed.

They walked out the back door to the boat moored at the dock. It was a beautiful vessel. He had Carol get in first and start the engine. The key was in the ignition, ready for the game to begin. Well, maybe continue.

Bobbie Lee cast off the lines, turned on the CB and motioned for his passenger to sit in the front seat. He slowly backed the boat away from the dock and headed for his prescribed location.

Carol had never been to the bayou before, but she wasn't stupid. The thought of jumping overboard and trying to swim to shore with alligators looking for a meal, was not in her plans.

As the boat motored the narrow waterway, the CB started crackling. "Breaker 19 for that lovely Chris Craft coming down Grand."

Bobbie was the only one visible, so whoever saw him, was asking to chat.

"What shall I say?" he asked Carol.

"Reply with some stupid handle, Bobbie Lee," she replied. "Have you never worked a CB before?"

Brilliant, but so dumb, she thought. Or maybe he was a CB virgin.

He was unable to come up with a good response.

"Damn, Bobbie Lee," she said walking back to the cockpit. "Give me the mike."

"Don't say anything stupid," he reminded her.

"Breaker 19, this is Cheese N Louise. Come back."

She did everything she could do to keep from laughing so hard and not fall overboard.

"Got that. Must be Louise. You be related to Mike and Mollie? Looks like his boat."

"10-4, Good Buddy," Carol said snickering.

Hell, if she was going to die today, she was going to have fun first.

"They out of town. Said we could zip around the backwater and do some sightseeing. Aunt Millie, she's a hoot."

"Got that right. Once she gets yapping, can't stop her You need help, stay on this channel. We out."

Carol put down the mike and went back to the stern.

"That was good," Bobbie Lee said nervously. "You behaved well."

Carol smiled but made no attempt to reply.

Chapter Forty-Nine - Showtime

"Breaker 5."

Moyes jumped up off his seat and scrambled to the CB. Roxie and Les heard the call from outside, and rushed in.

"Breaker 5, you got Moyes here."

"Why doesn't he use a handle?" Les asked Roxie.

Mount Moyes stood up and turned toward Les.

"Don't want one. Don't need one."

That was a perfectly reasonable explanation for Les.

"Moyes, this is Amos Moses up Chackbay. We got your Pillsbury, and he's carrying a delicious dumpling with him. He's in Mikey's boat."

"How do you know it wasn't Mikey?"

"Cause the little dumpling he's carrying thinks Millie is Mikey's wife."

Jesse and Moyes started laughing. Then Moyes got serious and turned to Les.

"Millie is Mikey's dog."

"Roger that. Keep an eye out. You gonna follow him?"

"Nah, he's going southeast. We pass it off to Betty Boop. And I told them to stay on 19, case they needed help."

"Smooth move, Amos. We thank ya. Out."

"Does Mr. Amos have only one arm?" Les asked. "You know, from the song?"

"Amos is his name. But he got a big old white beard like that other Moses character."

Roxie collected all her gear, which was sitting on the table. "Time to go," she said to Les.

"Linc, you're coming with us," Roxie said.

"Showtime," said Moyes. "Jesse, man the CB."

Les acted surprised. He didn't expect anyone else to get involved. This was a job for the FBI.

"Better if we split up," she said. "Mr. Boudin and I will go and get situated on land. You can perch yourself in a cove. You and Agent Michaels can go together."

Neither Les nor Moyes were happy with the arrangement, but they chose the lesser of two punishments, working together instead of contradicting Roxie. Roxie came up to Moyes and placed her hand on his arm. His shoulder was too far up there.

"There's no one else I want to get us through the bayou."

Roxie was right and Moyes, of course, agreed, but he wasn't about to say so.

"Miss Roxie, I always had your back. Not the time to quit now."

Death was coming, and it wasn't going back empty-handed. Like Moyes said, it was showtime and Death was sitting front row. Boudin had the boats running at idle outside at the docks. Roxie had her service weapon holstered to her side. Les carried a long slender bag. In it was his M40A1. Both had Kevlar vests. Moyes carried himself and a roll of duct tape on a carabiner attached to his belt.

Les looked at the tape and then up at Moyes. "Don't ask," Moyes advised.

As the group got into their assigned boats, Moyes asked. "Where're we going?"

Roxie pulled the coordinates from her head. "29.851 and 90.7."

Moyes looked at Les.

"Don't ask," Les advised.

Chapter Fifty – The Plan

The plan was simple. Let the prey float into the trap. The local gentry would then close off all routes. Wasn't hard down there. Just a few places in and out. Roxie would be hiding on land, since the prescribed coordinates were not on the water. Les would come in from behind Bobbie Lee's boat and disable it.

There would be distractions to separate the "dumpling" from Pillsbury. Bad guy caught. The girl saved. Fais-do-do. Sounded easy on paper, or in someone's head.

As Roxie and Boudin arrived at their place, she became concerned about the dumpling. From Amos Moses' description, she was the one communicating, not Bobbie Lee. Was there a Stockholm Syndrome thing happening? If so, then why were they going through with the plan?

But then again, Abraham had his son Isaac carry the firewood to his own sacrificial altar. Then there was a Moses, and Onan spilling his seed. Things were getting too Biblical. Roxie just hoped that Carol and Bobbie Lee didn't get to "know" each other in the Biblical sense.

Bobbie Lee took his gentle time down Grand Bayou. He stayed in the middle of the channel. Carol wondered where he got skilled in steering so well. She shrugged it off. She had no interest in getting to know Bobbie Lee personally.

They passed an old woman off the side fishing from her pirogue. She gave them a nice friendly wave. Bobbie Lee nodded. Carol made a big wide arc with both arms. Bobbie Lee didn't see her.

"Howdy," she yelled to the fisher lady.

"Good day for catching them bottom feeders," the woman yelled back.

The message was sent and received. After the boat passed out of sight, the fisher lady got on her CB.

"Breaker 5. Betty Boop hollerin'."

"Come back, Betty. This here Snake Girl."

"Well, child. Glad to have you back. Your papa be mighty glad you're ridding these waters of those predators."

Roxie would have loved to make a nice chat with Betty, but it was business time.

"Much obliged, Betty. What ya seein' out there?" Roxie asked.

The whole team was listening on Channel 5.

"Pillsbury just passed. The dumpling just gave me the distress signal."

Any boater would know it. Carol, somehow, knew it. It worked. And there couldn't have been a better definition for Bobbie Lee than a "bottom feeder". Roxie was relieved to know that Carol was not in on Bobbie Lee's plan. All the more reason to separate her.

"Was the dumpling looking good?" Roxie asked.

"For a dumpling, I would say so, but time's running out. They not far from their destination," came the reply.

"Breaker 5. Close the gates," Roxie instructed.

A flurry of responses flooded the airwaves at 27.015 MHz. Eugenie sat in the shade, tuned in to the proceedings. She wanted so much to wish them all good luck. Luck wasn't what they needed. They were looking for a mistake. Even Rudy seemed tense, sensing his master's emotions.

Bobbie Lee watched the GPS counting down the seconds of longitude as he approached from the west. Looking at the monitor, he decided this was the best place to run up on shore and start the walk. It was not far, once on land.

He slowly steered the boat onto shore, running into the soft mud, and giving it a little extra push to secure it. He reached down and pulled out his father's Mossberg 12 gauge wrapped in a blanket.

"What the hell is that for?" Carol asked.

"Security. These waters are filled with things that will eat you."

"How do you know all of this?"

"I planned this all out from the beginning. The coordinates are exact within a few seconds of latitude and longitude. I didn't particularly like having Position Nine down here, but it was worth studying it."

"Where are we going from here?"

"About 1509 feet south."

"About 1509?" Carol asked, puzzled. "You couldn't have said about 1500? Or about a fifth of a mile or maybe three football fields? Geez, Bobbie Lee."

"You asked."

Carol was beside herself. She was going to get murdered by a numbers nut.

He will probably cut me up into 64 pieces of equal weight with less than .003% deviation. What an ass.

"Do you expect me to carry anything? Maybe your big gun?"

Bobbie didn't catch the double entendre.

"Put these boots on. Where we are going, your Michael Kors flats are useless."

"Aww, you are so sweet, Bobbie Lee." Carol was shocked, impressed that the kid knew shoes. "How kind of you to think of me."

Bobbie Lee got out of the boat first, testing the sponginess of the ground. Firm. Nice. Good for walking.

Carol tarried in the boat. *I'm having a difficult time getting into these boots*, she thought. Function over fashion. They also smelled.

"Hurry up," he said.

"Yes, dear, just a moment while I check my hair."

Carol's probabilities of survival looked good at this point. Her plan to change the game was in place.

"Bobbie Lee, the boat is coming loose from the shore. What shall I do?"

The Damsel in Distress ploy always worked. She made herself easy for him, acted submissive, played the weaker sex.

Frustration, if measured with some bar graph, started approaching an uncomfortable Y value for him. As he approached the boat, he put one hand on the gunwale. Carol grabbed a rubber fender sitting inside the cockpit and slammed it against the side of his head, forcing him back to the ground, dazed.

She started the engine and threw the throttle in reverse. She had just enough time to get the boat out of the mud before he came to his senses and grabbed the shotgun.

She shoved the throttle causing the boat to lunge forward with a loud roar. She was free, until another loud sound rang in her ears and she was knocked down by pellets from a 12-gauge, peppering her left arm. It was all quiet after that. Yet the boat raced back upstream, guided by someone other than herself.

Bobbie Lee fired the other shot at the boat, but to no avail.

Chapter Fifty-One – The Crossroads

Roxie almost jumped out of her skin when she heard the blast of a gun in the near distance, just across a stand of trees. She remembered gun shots many years ago. A call for help? Or a call for the Doc? She didn't know.

Over the airwaves Channel 5 became a flurry of chatter. Sound traveled well down in the bayou. The thick air helped its movements across the water and over the cypress. Everyone heard it. Someone was in trouble.

"Hold your positions," Roxie screamed. "Les, Linc, what's your twenty?"

Moyes got on the CB while Les unpacked his rifle.

"About 200 yards from that blast. We may be east of it."

Mr. Boudin looked up to see a flock of herons escaping from the west of their position. They flew directly overhead.

"Good Lord sending our feathered friends to point us the way," he remarked.

"Stay in the boat, Mr. Boudin." Roxie advised. "And keep people informed as much as you can tell."

"You got that right." Boudin replied.

He was happy knowing he wasn't going in the line of fire with Snake Girl.

Bobbie Lee ran south along a narrow tributary. He had memorized the satellite view of his current position. This tributary crossed a well-defined cut in the trees. It was wide enough for vehicles to pass. This would be his escape. Follow the water far enough and it dumps out on Choctaw Road.

Les and Moyes continued up Grand Bayou and came to the place where Bobbie Lee and Carol ran aground. There was a knapsack sitting by the shore. No sign of Bobbie Lee, Carol, or the boat.

"He had to go south along this narrow channel," Moyes said. "It leads to the main road and out of the bayou."

"How far?" Les asked.

"About a mile as the crow flies. Maybe a little less."

"Won't take him long to get there. We need to hurry. Can we get down this channel on this boat?"

"Might. Got a shallow draft. We stay in the center, we be okay. Just take it slow. He ain't getting out."

Les didn't want to ask Moyes how he knew that, but he was impressed at the large man's calm demeanor under such times of stress.

Bobbie Lee heard a boat come down the channel. He checked his inventory of rounds. Four shells for the shotgun. He loaded two of them. He was angry that he wasted one on that bitch in the boat. There were six rounds left in the .45.

He was about thirty yards from the boat. Using the shotgun in these trees was not going to work. Twenty yards was a good range with the handgun. Bobbie Lee fired, shattering the bow rail. Moyes and Les hit the deck as metal and wood flew all around them.

"Count the rounds, if you can," Les said in a whisper as they huddled as low as possible. "He should have five left. Six if he didn't have one in the chamber."

Moyes was not in the mood to do any kind of counting. He was figuring out how to reach the throttle and back his black butt out of there.

Another shot pierced the bow. Moyes reached up and shoved the throttle in reverse.

"Run it aground," Les said. "So, I can get out of this thing."

Moyes did as he asked but put a little distance in between him and the shooter first. When the stern hit mud, Les jumped out and crouched behind a big cypress. With the scope on his rifle, Les was unable to see the shooter. He was probably lying low, too. Moyes stayed in the boat.

Roxie found the clearing just as the shots rang out to the west of her. She started running. *Who would get to the clearing first?* she wondered.

Eugenie sat on the edge of her chair listening to the chatter. People talking, sending mixed signals. She had to play the mother now.

"Breaker 5. This is Honey Bee. Maintain radio silence until we get an all clear."

The CBs from all over the bayou started clicking. There was no talking. They were all just keying the mikes. It was a sign of acknowledgment. A silent 10-4. Then it all went quiet.

Pere Chastain had his orders given to him at The Meeting. At the first sign of gunfire, call the Sheriff's Department. He did. They were on their way. Doc Ribeau was also called, in case someone got scraped up, or worse.

Chapter Fifty-Two ~ The Dumpling

"Breaker 9. We have an emergency."

"That you, Betty Boop?"

"Roger that. We have a shotgun victim, female."

"10-20?"

"On Grand Bayou. Stand by for coordinates."

"10-4."

"29.854 and 90.702. You will see Mikey's boat. Just up in the loop. In the channel."

"We know right where that is. Can you give us a status of the victim?"

"Shotgun wounds to the left arm and side. I have bleeding under control, but she goes in and out of consciousness."

"We have a boat on the way."

"10-4. Out."

Betty Boop stopped fishing when the sounds of gunfire were heard. She was a retired Army nurse and did not pack up her things and motor off to safer waters. She hurried downstream where she found Mikey's boat that had run aground, engine still running.

She pulled up next to the Chris Craft and saw the woman who sent the distress signal earlier, lying in the bottom of the cockpit, bleeding. Betty hopped across the boats and began ripping up a blanket that lay on one of the seats and used it for bandages.

"You're gonna be alright, Hon," she said, comforting Carol.

Carol regained consciousness enough to feel a warm touch and excruciating pain. She opened her eyes and saw the fisher lady in the boat with her.

"Save Indie," Carol whispered just before she passed out again.

Betty felt Carol's pulse. It was still there.

"No problem, Child. Indie will be okay."

Betty didn't know an Indie, but she did recognize a nice pair of Michael Kors flats, even though they were probably no longer any good due to all the blood.

"Breaker 5. The dumpling is safe."

Betty heard mikes getting keyed up in "silent" response to the good news.

Eugenie heard the message also and rejoiced at Betty's report. She switched to Channel 9 to see if she could catch any more information. She hoped for the safety of the others out there, the others facing Death watching from the front row.

Les could finally see movement from his scope. The trees were thick in that area, but if he saw Bobbie Lee, he could get a good shot. Just needed that right moment. The seconds passed like a lifetime. When the movement settled, Les put his finger on the trigger, took in a deep breath and let it out, then pulled.

Roxie stopped dead in her tracks. She recognized the report from an M40A1. Many days were spent on the firing range at Quantico trying all the arsenal the agency possessed. Today was not target practice.

Les looked in his scope and saw no movement. "Bobbie Lee?" he yelled.

There was no answer.

"FBI, Bobbie Lee. Give yourself up. The game is over."

No response.

"You think you got him?" asked Moyes still huddled in the bottom of the boat.

Les stood up to get a higher angle still using the scope on his rifle to see. But sometimes looking through the scope gives too myopic a view of the world. He didn't see Bobbie Lee standing about ten yards to his right until it was too late.

The blasts from the Mossberg caught Les in the vest and lower part of his leg, which was not as protected. The force of the pellets knocked him and his rifle into the channel.

Moyes could hear Roxie screaming from the south. So did Bobbie Lee. He threw the shotgun down knowing it would take too long to reload and ran toward the sound of her voice.

Moyes looked up to see that Bobbie Lee had gone through the trees. *He better be armed if he's fixin' to run into Roxie*, he thought.

Les lay on his back about 50 feet down the channel from the boat. Part of him was still in the water. His leg burned from the buckshot, and he slowly raised his head to see where Moyes was. His vest was up around his face and throat and all he could muster was a half-hearted yell.

Good thing he wasn't alone, for he heard rustling of sticks and splashes of water nearby. Bad thing it wasn't Moyes. A gator slowly crept up on Les. After all, it was lunch time. Les didn't have his rifle, and his sidearm had shifted around and underneath him.

That's why my left rear felt uncomfortable, he thought. Les didn't like the fact that after all this trouble to get Bobbie Lee, he was going to be eaten. Death didn't know refreshments were being served in that front row. *Damn.*

"Moyes?" Les yelled or tried to. "Need your help here."

The gator was getting close to Les' leg. Didn't help that his blood was seasoning the air and water for the gator. But in his discomfort and pain, he thought he saw an eclipse. It was Moyes.

Moyes crept up on the gator and sat down on his back, took the gator's large mouth and closed it with one hand. Gators have an incredible bite force of a few thousand pounds. Not something you want your leg to feel. But their jaws don't have a lot opening force. This one wasn't amused that his "Happy Meal" was being postponed.

Moyes took the duct tape off the carabiner hanging from his belt and pulled off a few feet. He then wrapped the gator's mouth with the tape and sat there smiling at Les.

"Moyes, I'm not gonna ask," Les said as he passed out.

Moyes brought a length of rope with him and tied the gator to a tree, so he could pick up the limp agent back to the boat.

"Breaker 9."

"Is this an emergency?"

"FBI agent shot, near the prescribed coordinates."

"We have a medical team on the Grand not far from you, tending to another gunshot victim. Betty Boop heading to your twnety as we speak."

"10-4. Can anyone relay this report? They listening on 5. Pillsbury is on foot, heading toward Snake Girl."

"We'll get a call in."

Moyes was not aware of another victim since he and Les had gone down the channel. He figured it was "Dumpling".

Eugenie heard Moyes' call on channel 9, and her heart jumped. Les was shot and tears filled her eyes. She switched back to channel 5 to a frenzy of chatter.

"Breaker 5. Honey Bee here, where is Snake Girl?"

Boudin picked up the mike.

"Blackjack here, Miss Bee. Snake Girl heading toward her partner. She gonna go full throttle on Pillsbury's ass if she finds him. But she ain't carrying a handheld, so she don't know what's happening."

"Her partner took a shot to his leg. Moyes has him."

"Damn. There be hell to pay for this."

When Betty arrived to care for Les before the medic team came down, Moyes turned the agent over to her.

"Gotta let a friend loose."

"Do what you need to do, Moyes. I got the agent," Betty said.

Moyes was quietly singing to himself. He was going to the crossroads, asking the Lord to save poor Bob.

The gator didn't move much, having been tied to a tree. Probably embarrassing for him. Moyes came up from behind and sat down on his back and cut the duct tape off his mouth. The gator opened his jaws wide and gave a horrible hiss and grunt. Moyes slowly backed off, untied the rope, and the gator hightailed it into the water.

Chapter Fifty-Three ~ A Second Grave

Roxie ran along the wide clearing in the trees trying to reach Les, focusing on the direction where she last heard the gunshot. The clearing dead ended at the channel. Did she want to yell for Les and give away her position or did she prefer to lay low and let Bobbie Lee walk into her sights.

She was out of breath and stopped to hear something. Anything. All the fussing and shooting scared away the birds and land creatures, so there was little natural noise to confuse her. She pulled out her service weapon and held it face level scanning her surroundings.

Roxie needed information. She had no radio. She didn't know how Carol was, where she was. She didn't have a clue who was in the way of the latest shotgun blasts. No sign of Les or Moyes. Were they hurt? Linc was so big, an easy target. *Please not him. Please not Les.* Where was Bobbie Lee?

Then she remembered she was in the bayou, in the backwater, in the special part of God's vineyard.

Slow down. Be like the water. She lowered her pistol and took a deep breath and closed her eyes for a moment. She thought of Pere Remy. What would he do? How would he handle this mess? Then she envisioned the moccasin and the empty pirogue, the sadness, and the anger of being torn from her home to go live in Houston, of all places.

"Drop the gun, Agent." Bobbie Lee said from behind her.

She froze in place, slowly raised her arms out and dropped her weapon.

"That you, Bobbie Lee?"

"How did you know I was going to be here?" he asked. "You were never a part of this game. All those who knew it are dead. You weren't supposed to be here."

Roxie knew when a person was showing a certain emotion. She didn't have to see his face to know he was frustrated by the current situation, disappointed that his brilliant plan had failed. And especially that he would not be able to finish, since the last two Dotties were safe.

"I like puzzles myself, Bobbie Lee," she said teasing him.

"But the game has come to an end, and you lost."

Roxie could hear a distinctive click. He just took off the safety.

"You're a troubled young man," she added. "I can help you."

Roxie could say those things and mean it, having spent years in these woods helping trouble youth.

"Did you notice, Agent," he replied. "I'm the one holding the cards?"

"My name is Roxie."

Time to personalize the situation.

"I get why you killed these girls. They embarrassed you, humiliated you. Been there."

"You don't know me or anything about me!"

"I'm here, aren't I?"

Bobbie Lee slowly walked around Roxie and kept the gun pointing at her face, until he stood straight in front of her. At a safe distance, of course. He didn't notice that she shifted her feet into her Wing Chun stance: feet shoulder width, toes pointing to a spot about a yard in front of her. Now she felt balanced.

"How did you know I was here? Who told you?"

"No one that you knew. It was a simple puzzle that some autistic kid solved. He saw the dates and locations."

"You're a liar. She told you."

"I tracked you down, I saw the game, your incredible use of numbers and math and order and skill in planning. I am impressed. But why the flaws, Bobbie Lee?"

When you're gonna die, it's always nice to throw in some compliments to your killer, she pondered.

"What flaws? It was a well-designed plan."

"The coordinates. They are off."

"Margin of error."

"Hmm. Mathematicians don't do margin of error. Calculation are perfect, absolute."

"You're correct, but math only works perfectly in nature. Throw humans into the equation, and you have to fudge things to get them to work. Almost is good enough, they say."

"But they're wrong, aren't they?"

"You're FBI. Probably have a degree in Psychology." Bobbie Lee paused for a second. "You're here profiling me. Well, isn't that something?"

He slowly walked around her like a moon to its mother planet.

"What I don't get, Bobbie Lee, is your father. It deviated from your normal pattern. It was inconsistent with your behavior. Everyone else was a woman."

"My father left me with her," he said as his rage started leaking out of his pores. "If he had made her happy and did what he should have done, she would not have hurt me."

He was thinking of Mother.

"She did things that were not appropriate."

"I must say, castrating him was a creative move, messy though."

"It was the perfect way to go."

"Then what about the other women? Why the boot to the throat?"

Roxie knew why. She just wanted to hear it from him.

"They talk too much. They laughed. You can't laugh when your throat is smashed."

Roxie noticed the present tense on "talk" and past tense on "laughed".

"No one is laughing anymore, Bobbie Lee."

"Amanda is laughing."

"Why wasn't she first?" Roxie asked.

Might as well get all the questions out there before he pulls the trigger.

"Seems like she hurt you the most."

"She excited me the most. It was all the others who saw me after it happened."

Roxie was not expecting that reply.

"Look, Bobbie Lee. I am not a part of your game. I'm on the outside of your nine dots. You have already drawn the lines. The pencil doesn't go through me."

Bobbie Lee walked slowly around toward the front of Roxie and lowered his gun pointing it to her chest.

"You're afraid, aren't you? Afraid a bullet will go through you instead of a pencil."

"Yes, I am afraid, but not like the others you killed. Were they afraid?"

"Doesn't matter."

"I'm afraid of this world losing another brilliant mind. We're running out of them these days."

"Good, Ms. Psychologist," he said smirking. "Trying to butter me up, make me give in. Aww, you want my gun, Agent Roxie?"

"Yes. I want the game to end."

Bobbie Lee yelled at the top of his lungs, "I'M NOT FINISHED!"

He quickly glanced around, just in case he spoke too loudly. "This way."

He pointed his gun toward the north from where he came.

"What do you want from me, Bobbie Lee? I'm not a game piece. I'm not just a number."

"Shut up."

Bobbie Lee was thinking. She was not in his plan. She was a defect in the game.

"May I lower my arms? They're getting tired. And where are we going?"

He nodded, and she put her arms to her side and tightened her fists. Roxie tilted her head over to the channel that Bobbie Lee was standing in front of.

"We need to finish this part of the game."

"You mean at the proper coordinates? That will take you right into the path of the others out there waiting for you."

Bobbie Lee inched slowly toward Roxie. He had the gun. He was in charge, but he was at a loss.

"Looks like we are at the crossroads, she said. "The water channel right here, crossing the wide vehicle path over there. You know about the crossroads, don't you? You killed the Dotties at the crossroads."

"Great song."

He ignored the part about the killing.

"Were you named after him? After Robert Johnson?"

"If you knew my Mother, you would probably think she sold me to the Devil. Maybe she was right."

Then he started to hum a song and spoke the words, "Nobody seem to know me, babe, everybody passed me by."

"Someone noticed you." Roxie said in a sadly sympathetic tone, thinking of Indira. *Poor child*, she thought.

Bobbie Lee began to lower his gun. He was pondering those he had left to kill. The girl with the 31 on her hand, and the woman who made him feel alive.

Bobbie Lee made a mistake. He let a woman get in his head. Let her scent dance in the smell receptors of his mind, let the brain calculate her curves and her form in all her delicious beauty. He became the sailor being beckoned by the Sirens on the rocks. Well, one Siren.

Roxie's tension had built up to the level she needed, and she swung her right hand toward his wrist holding the gun as her left hand swooped in to twist the gun out of his hand. She was quick, but the gun went off. The concussion wave blew her hair back, and she felt the bullet slam into her clavicle, shattering it. The force ripped her back and with it his gun. She landed backward on the ground and the momentum of the fall carried the gun past her.

Bobbie Lee made no effort to consult Moyes about how close he should get to Roxanne Cormier. She stood up as quick as she could, and front kicked him directly at the pubic symphysis shattering his pelvis in two. The force caused him to lurch forward as he screamed in pain. A second well-placed side kick caught him below his chin, crushing his windpipe with such force that it knocked him back on the soft mud shore of the channel. She could hear his gurgling as he struggled for a breath.

Roxie fell back to the ground. The pain wasn't something they taught at Quantico. She heard voices coming from the north. Voices shouting her name.

Roxie screamed, "Over here. On the clearing."

The voices were getting closer. She would be saved. Not so much for Bobbie Lee. As he lay there taking his last breath, a gator surfaced next to him, opened its jaws, and clamped down on Bobbie Lee's head, dragging his body into the brown brackish water.

There was no need to shoot the gator. Bayou knew how to clean up the mess. Poor gator just wanted lunch. Roxie sat in awe as she watched Bobbie Lee's lifeless body disappear. She didn't turn her head. That would have hurt too much. She didn't get sick at the sight of a gator munching a human. Well, later she got sick after the shock of the whole event wore off.

Moyes sped down the channel and stopped in the clearing, surprised to see just Roxie. He saw two guns lying on the ground and wondered.

"Where's Pillsbury?" he asked.

"Gator got him. Where's Les? Is he okay?"

"Damn. Must've been the one I did a catch-and-release on. Yeah, Agent Michaels took a gun blast to the leg. The Dumpling got a blast in the arm. They both gonna pull through."

"Can you help me? I've been shot." Roxie pleaded.

Moyes jumped out of the boat and ran, well, lumbered toward her. He gently removed the Kevlar vest, as she reeled in pain.

"No blood," he said. "But that bullet sure slammed into you."

He took out a knife and cut open her shirt at the shoulder.

"Bayou smiling down on you, Miss Roxie. Hell. It just a compression wound. The vest stopped the bullet but not the force."

Roxie looked at her heavily bruised shoulder. She was bleeding on the inside and the collar bone was definitely shattered.

"Let's get you into town, get you looked at."

"Can you drive me?" she asked.

"How bout we call it 'Driving Miss Roxie.'"

"A little stereotypical, don't you think?"

"Hon, I know you're injured and all that. But I'm close enough for you to lay a Wing Chun on me, but ain't no way I'm labeling you the old white woman sittin' in the back."

"I heard Les get off a shot. You tellin' me he missed?"

Moyes just laughed as he put Miss Roxie in the boat.

"No, ma'am. He was dead center. Only problem Pillsbury wasn't in the shirt that is now well ventilated. Kid was smart. Gotta give ya that. How did Pillsbury buy it? Well, besides the gator buffet, I mean."

"Front kick to the pelvis, side kick to the throat."

Moyes didn't respond. He placed Roxie as far back in the boat as he could. He decided to make a mental note to draw up a sign that would be placed in the lobby of Moyes Swamp Tours. It would read, "Kindly stay more than ten feet from the black-haired Acadian, Roxanne Cormier."

Roxie lay in the back of the boat as Moyes headed for Grand Bayou. The flood of all that happened came crashing down on her. Bobbie Lee, the victims. She put it all together and muttered, *Hmm, Great minds die alike.* Death left the front row. Wasn't the ending it expected. Dinner and a movie, it thought. Not bad.

Chapter Fifty-Four – The Laptop

Roxie had surgery on her shoulder to repair her clavicle which was broken by Bobbie Lee's close-range shot. A few plates, some screws, and nice painkillers later., she was back in her office, arm in a sling. Les was still recovering from the shotgun blast. He needed knee surgery, so he wasn't getting around much for a while.

Roxie was pleased to know that not many people were there on July 3. They decided to enjoy a long holiday weekend. She needed to do some paperwork after all the fuss in the bayou.

Eddie Lamping walked in and dropped Bobbie Lee's laptop on her desk. He was one of the IT Geeks assigned to check out the contents inside.

"His laptop has some weird encryption on it," Eddie said frustrated. "They can't seem to get in unless they have his password. When they entered the fourth wrong password, the laptop locked up. The only way to try again was to reboot the system, which seemed to reset the counter. I'm returning the laptop to you, to see if you might have any other ideas, maybe clues from his life would help."

Roxie looked at the laptop sitting there, taunting her to be opened.

"Sure. I will take a try."

Eddie walked off. He had holiday plans. Roxie got on the phone.

"Michaels."

"Cormier. How are you feeling?"

"Like I've been shot. And you?"

"Like I've been shot."

"Okay, now that the small talk is over, why did you call? Don't tell me you're working so soon."

"I have Bobbie Lee's laptop and I'm dying to get into it."

"Can you use some word beside 'dying'?"

"Funny. Um, we can't break into the computer. We need a password. Were there any telltale signs in his room to give us a clue? Anything?"

"Not that I can remember. It was all so sterile. No clutter, nothing out of place. There were no posters on the walls, no trophies."

"He was a Math whiz. He must have used some code or obscure formula, or a name. IT tried Elbert, Shirley, Bobbie and then all the names backwards. They tried all the famous Blues singers. They went to famous Mathematicians: Euler, Newton, Gauss, Pythagoras. Nothing worked."

"His birthplace?" Les asked. "Wisconsin Badgers."

"Let me give it a try." Roxie opened the laptop and turned it on. The operating system came up in Windows 7. "Hmm, he didn't even upgrade to 10 yet."

The login screen already had the username displayed. Now it was waiting for a password. Roxie reviewed all the entries previously made, reviewed what she remembered seeing in his house, mentally gathered the names of his victims and the game he was playing.

Roxie entered the name of each woman he brutally murdered. After the fourth try, the system locked up. She cursed quietly and waited for a reboot.

"What was Fibonacci's first name?" she asked.

"I don't know. Let me look it up."

Roxie could hear Les over the phone struggling to get up out of bed or some comfortable chair. A moment later he came back.

"Fibonacci was a nickname. It meant Son of Bonacci."

Roxie tried "Fibonacci", "Bonacci", and both names backwards. Locked. Time to reboot. Then she remembered what her father told her as she was on their final adventure. To see something and make a name for it. Something that only made sense to her to get back, as a landmark.

She "sat on the hot stove" waiting for the next login prompt. When the cursor blinked tempting her for another try, she typed in "F1b0n@cc1". There was no "Incorrect Password" message this time. The computer logged her into Bobbie Lee's desktop.

"We're in."

"Excellent. How did you do it?"

"Auntie Hazel's mole."

"I don't want to know."

Roxie found a video chat application and opened a session with Les. As he watched, she scrolled through the files under the Documents folder. All the file names were date-stamped. There was a folder for each year and a subfolder for each month of the year.

Roxie picked a file with a recognizable name: 2014_10_29.enc. She was prompted by the operating system that it could not open the file.

"Looks like all the files are encrypted. Maybe that is what the .enc file suffix means," she said.

"Open a command window and type 'decrypt'. Maybe he has his own encryption tool on here," advised Les.

"You think it is that easy?"

"Occam's Razor."

"What?"

"Just try it."

Roxie opened a command window like Les suggested and entered "decrypt". The program returned a message asking for a file name. Roxie copied the full path to the ".enc" file. A short moment after, the program stopped, and a new file appeared on the desktop: 2014_10_29.txt.

"Brilliant, Les. Let's see what's inside. Probably a journal entry for that date."

2014 29 October – Found Mother in the basement. She was lying wrong. Fixed her position. Poor Mother. Did not see the wire. Plan worked. 911 called. Removed wire. Police came. Asked the wrong questions. EMT slipped carrying stretcher up the stairs. Tried not to laugh. Acted like the poor orphan.

"Incroyable. It is all here. Everything he did he recorded it. What is the date of Math Camp? He has to have an entry from then."

"Camp was from July 13, 2009 to July 18, but we know he wasn't there the whole time."

"There's a file dated 2009_07_17. That has to be it."
Roxie ran the decrypting code on the file and opened it up.

2009 17 July – Mother wanted to know the reason for coming home early. Mother wanted to know why there were less clothes than what she packed. Where were the new jeans? A pair of underwear was missing. Took a shower four times. Mother wanted to know why so many times showering. They all laughed. They all did this. They will pay.

"This was a revenge killing, but he couldn't even put into words what happened to him."

"It must have been traumatic, beyond just a prank. A kid like that having to explain why he had some sexual experience gone wrong at a place where no one expected it to happen."

Roxie and Les spent the next two hours decrypting all the files on the laptop, reading the journal entries of a troubled soul. They went through his emails, looked under the Trash folder. Empty. Sent Items Folder. Empty. They found some images from Math Camp, pictures of the Nine Dotties gathered working on their projects together.

"How did he get these?" Roxie asked.

"Someone obviously sent them to him," Les said.

It was obvious, because there was never a mention of Bobbie Lee hanging around them taking snapshots. Roxie had opened the images in GIMP 2, which Bobbie had been using. The images were broken up into layers and Roxie viewed one of them.

"Mon Dieu."

Chapter 55 – Position 5

Indira Gamal just returned from San Diego. She had received the call from Agent Cormier, saying the problem was fixed. There was no longer any need to fear. While she was trying to get her life back in order, there was a knock at the door, and Indira answered it.

"What the hell are you doing here?"

A tall voluptuous woman stood at the door, looking disheveled after a long drive.

"Indie, aren't you glad to see me?" Amanda Horsch asked. "It's all over."

"Why weren't you first, you slut?"

"Indie, Indie, calm down." Amanda was angry, but she tried to hide it. Friend to friend, you know. Although she didn't like to be called a slut. "May I come in?"

"I don't—"

Too late. Amanda burst inside, looking around at the clean furnishings and brightness of the walls.

"Nice place, you have, Indie. You did well."

Amanda didn't have those luxuries. Her riches came in praises of good looks over the counter, drooling truckers, jealous servers. But those riches didn't pay her bills.

"Not so much for you, huh, Manda?"

"Well, life is what it is. It's just a game."

"The game you played got six of our friends killed."

Amanda was good in math, but she was confused about the number six. Should have been seven, she thought.

"Games need to be completed, Indie. I'm here to finish it."

Indira took a few steps back, not expecting Amanda to get right to the point. What? No request for tea or coffee, or nice chocolates from an expensive store?

"Let's go into the living room and talk about this."

"Oh, now you're being civil. Sure."

Indira led Amanda into the living room. Two other women were sitting in chairs as Indira welcomed her old friend in for a chat. One woman had a bandage on her left arm; the other woman's arm was in a sling. It did not take much for Amanda to show her surprise.

"Carol? I thought you were dead." To Roxie. "Agent Cormier, why are you here?"

Two police officers from Boise PD came in and stood by the entrance to the living room, hands on their service revolvers. Roxie motioned for them to stand down.

"What is this all about?" Amanda asked.

"You are under arrest for the attempted murder of Indira Gamal, for being an accessory to the murders of Pei Leung, Annie Rhodes, Ginger Tervil, Jennifer France, Wendy Stern, Stacy Eddings, and an accessory to the attempted murder of Carol Marsh," Roxie explained.

"Wait a second. You're not going to pin all this on me. I was targeted also. That little Momma's boy couldn't find me. I was off his grid."

"Liar," Carol screamed. "You and I were a couple. You loved doing it with me."

"Well, girls know what girls like."

"But all you eventually talked about was Bobbie Lee this and Bobbie Lee that."

"What was special about Bobbie Lee?" Indira asked.

"Oh, Indie, Indie. You had no idea," Amanda explained.

"You didn't feel him getting aroused. That kid was not only blessed with a brilliant mind, but brilliant measurements. That was not a slide rule in his pants."

"That's sick," Carol said disgusted.

"That's because you like women. I took both sides. Whatever was best for me. And he had the size I wanted. But this little twerp couldn't control himself. Not then, at least."

"What the hell does that mean?" asked Indira.

Roxie stepped in on the argument. "We found it all, Ms. Horsch. We found all the emails and pictures you sent him. All the notes. The times you arranged to come see him in Wisconsin."

Amanda was incredulous.

"How did you find that stuff? He said all the files were encrypted. All the images were encrypted, the hidden texts safe."

"Good job at hiding your emails. They were placed in layers found in the GIF files you sent him. Innocuous pictures of Math Camp. Pictures of the Nine Dotties. Seemingly harmless. But the texts were readable when you changed opacity on the layers."

Amanda looked like she was going to faint. She sat down in a chair in the corner. The two police officers flanked her.

"He eventually liked it," she said.

"Liked what?" Carol asked.

"The sex. I shaped him into a man. He overcame his popping too quickly. I got what I wanted, and it was good, incredible. He had already offed Pei. I knew I couldn't stop him. He had a plan."

"You bitch. You could've stopped him," Indira shouted, crying. "For what? Just a simple prank?"

Amanda was past feeling. She used sex to escape. Look where it got her. Might as well paint "Slut, Whore-sch. For a Good Time, Call" on her again. It no longer mattered.

"You were the one who kept in touch secretly with all the Nine Dotties," said Roxie. "You found out where they were living. The delectable Amanda coerced them into meeting you. Let's catch up on old times, you said."

"I was never involved in his killings." Amanda said trying to justify her actions.

"Didn't matter. You led him to them, like lambs to the slaughter."

"Lambs? Yeah right. All of you got your kicks watching me seduce him. Not an innocent one among you."

"I did everything I could do to stop you. You know that," said Indira.

"Yeah, well, I couldn't allow you to enjoy his physical gift."

"And what about his parents?" asked Carol. "Where did they fit in your plan?"

"Hey, sweetie," Amanda said, defensively. "They were his own doing. Sounds like his parents deserved what they got. They treated him like crap."

"No one deserves to die." Roxie said.

"There are worse things than death."

"Did you arrange for the boat in Chackbay? In Louisiana?" asked Roxie.

"Yeah, I called in a favor. Some trucker from down there had a nice power boat. A Chris Craft. Said it would take the bayous quite well."

"And what was your part of the deal?"

"The girls." Amanda cupped her breasts. "I told you in Limon, they were all I had."

Carol remembered Amanda's girls, too. One time in her life, they were all she could think about and enjoy. Now, they only sickened her.

"So, Manda," Indira said shaking feverishly. "Why are you here? To finish off what Bobbie Lee started?"

Amanda looked around the room. She was going nowhere. She was not going to finish the job Bobbie Lee started. Amanda could not speak. Nothing went well for her in her life. And this was no exception. She was to be pitied.

Obviously, Bobbie Lee was gone. They were supposed to meet together after he finished off Indira. She sat there realizing that she no longer had her audience at Verl's Diner. The thought of Peggy taking her place made her sick. The killings didn't affect her, but Peggy at the counter?

Indira stood up and walked over to Amanda who had her head down. She touched her on her shoulder, as Amanda looked up. No tears. No regrets.

Indira looked sadly into her former friend's empty stare, "Well, as Bill Paxton said in "Aliens": 'Game Over, Man.'"

The two officers grabbed Amanda by the arms and lifted her up. One of them began, "You have the right to remain silent—"

The rest of what the sad woman heard was a blur.

Chapter Fifty-Six ~ The Ceremony

Agent Michaels put in a request to the Section Manager. The Section Manager approved it and sent it on to the General Services Administration, the agency that oversees the facilities of Federal buildings. The Regional Director of the GSA thought it was a simple unassuming request, considering the circumstances. It was approved.

Odie Lanham arrived at the FBI Office with the sirens blaring. His idea. He was dressed in his Sunday best, compliments of his loving parents, although the sirens were a little too much, they thought. George and Suzanne Lanham escorted their son into the building and up to the third floor. As they got off the elevator, a crowd had already been assembled. They had collected in one of the hallways. There were about thirty happy smiling faces.

Odie recognized every one of them, except two women. One had long black hair and a henna tattoo on her right hand. The other was doing everything she could to hold back her tears. She had her left arm in bandages. Odie didn't know why she was hurt, but he had compassion for her. Wasn't the first time he was bandaged up.

When he saw Roxie and Les, his eyes beamed like a lighthouse beacon. He hurried up to them as they hugged him.

"What is all this about?" Odie asked.

Roxie looked over at George Lanham as he gestured something like it being a surprise.

"Odie, we have a surprise for you," Les said.

"Oh, Agent Les, I like surprises. Cake is always good."

The whole crowd laughed at the innocence standing before them. They weren't used to innocence. Their jobs were immersed in just the opposite. But not today, not for these few minutes.

"Odie, I would like you to meet some new people," Roxie said, motioning the two strangers to come. "This is Indira Gamal, and this is Carol Marsh."

Indira came up to Odie and gave him a big hug. "Thank for you all that you are," she said.

Carol took Odie's hand and then kissed him on the cheek. "You saved my life. I can never repay you. Thank you."

Odie never remembered saving anyone's life. He was confused. He saw the 31 tattooed on Indira's hand and the bandages on Carol. He looked at his parents, then to Les and finally to Roxie. Some place inside his head was hurting. He was missing some information.

Roxie came up to Odie and put her arm around him. "You saved these women's lives, Odie, by solving that puzzle on the whiteboard."

Odie looked sad. His smile had gone. It was just a puzzle, he thought. Just a puzzle. Just some dates on a whiteboard. Then he remembered what Roxie said. Something about finding someone. Odie's smile returned.

"You found them, didn't you!" he asked. "You found the ones who were lost."

Roxie, with tears beginning to form, replied, "You found them, Mr. Lanham. That is why were all here."

Roxie looked over toward the crowd as they parted, revealing a bright blue ribbon stretching across the hallway. Another stranger stood on the other side of the ribbon. He motioned for Odie and his parents to come forth. The Lanhams took their son and led him up to the stranger, a well-dressed man carrying a large pair ofscissors.

"On behalf of the General Services Administration and this Regional Office of the FBI, I hereby declare the hallway behind me the 'Odie R. Lanham Corridor'."

The well-dressed stranger then handed the young man the scissors, and Odie cut the ribbon. The crowd cheered and shouted. There were tears and laughing, hugs and handshakes. Roxie led Odie through the crowd past the ribbon and to a plaque down the hall. It read "For Meritorious Service Given by Odekirk Roy Lanham, to the Federal Bureau of Investigation".

"Miss Roxie, I don't know what to say," Odie whispered. "I didn't expect this."

"There are times in our lives, Mr. Lanham, that come as surprises. This is one of them," Roxie explained.

"Is there cake?"

Chapter Fifty-Seven – The Promotion

Bo, the convenience store manager, watched the evening news. There was a short insignificant mention of the happenings at the FBI building. Bo heard of the ceremony honoring his "Straightener".

The next day, Liz the gum chewing, nail primping cashier was let go. Bo called Odie in and promoted him to Liz's former position. People enjoyed doing business at the convenience store from then on. Customers would come in, testing the non-descript employee's knowledge of where things were.

"Powdered doughnuts?"

"Aisle A, third shelf, section 2."

"Aspirin?"

"Aisle C, top shelf, section 5."

Some wise guy came in seeing how far he could go with this kid. "Horse Chow?"

Odie stopped for a brief second, long enough for his synapses to fire across the appropriate network.

"You're just funning me. Refrigerator Section, Produce, Aisle D, first case."

The stunned prankster went to the exact place. There, sitting right where Odie said, was a package of precut apple slices.

"Horses love apples."

Chapter Fifty-Eight – Cake

The late August air hung like a wet blanket over a clothesline, thick and heavy. Down the channel at the Douillard home, Eugenie and Roxie sat outside amid the glow of citronella candles and bathed in whatever the box fans could provide. Rudy found solace in front of his own fan. The sun was still above the horizon but below the tree level. It shed a honey yellow glow to the place where two old friends talked.

"Does it still hurt?" Eugenie asked.

Roxie squirmed a little in her chair, trying to get more comfortable before answering. "Sometime, when I overexert myself, the shoulder talks to me," she replied. "I feel like a TV cop who got shot."

"What on earth?" Eugenie asked.

"You know how cops on TV always get shot in the shoulder."

The two women sat there and laughed, thinking the absurd.

"He was a sick young man, wasn't he?" Eugenie asked, thinking maybe Roxie could get it all out of her, like sucking venom out of your arm.

"Yeah. The kid gave in to the powers of sex. He was doomed from the beginning," Roxie replied.

Eugenie knew the power of sex. The extreme highs and devastating lows. Her husband pleased her well, and then he left, well he was eaten, leaving her with nothing. But she was a lady and wouldn't discuss it with Roxie. She just fanned herself.

Eugenie was not sure where Roxie stood on the subject. At that time, and in that place, it really didn't matter.

"Embarrassment and humiliation were a great power. It drove him to do unspeakable things, it seems." Eugenie felt sorry for him.

"He dug two graves." Roxie said trying to get comfortable with her shoulder.

"Pardon?"

"Confucius said, 'Before you embark on a journey of revenge, dig two graves'."

"A whole generation lost. A family tree at the end of its branch. Speaking of family." Eugenie broke the gloom in the topic. "You have a lot of kids coming tomorrow for their weeklong adventure. Can you handle it?"

"I will ignore it, like I always do." Although Roxie was not really sure this time. "Life goes on, you know," mused Roxie.

"Having the kids come before school starts is a change from the usual. Any reason for that?"

"The superintendent thought that it would be a good start for them. Maybe it would scare them into school, and they would be motivated to stay."

"I agree. That does seem to have some merit. Heard from Agent Michaels lately?"

"That was a quick change of subject, Eugenie."

"Come on. We're girls. Always nice to talk about boys."

"I thought we were ladies."

"Let ya hair down, Cher, for just a bit."

"Well, we keep in touch. He is now in the Seattle Office. They heard of his work on the Johnson case. There was an opening. He took it."

"And his leg?"

"He is walking without a cane now. A good sign."

"Too bad you two didn't hit it off."

"Just wasn't meant to be at this time. Hey, why are you asking me all about this? You have some gleam in your eye. What is going on?"

"Well, if you must pry, my dear. Mr. Jeremiah Aberdeen wants to come calling."

"Mon dieu, Eugenie." Roxie sat up straight, maybe too quickly.

"You mean Aberdeen as in Aberdeen Honey House up the road?"

"That be him."

"Well, I'll be. How on earth?"

"Poor man wanted to find out why his business was thriving all of a sudden. Mr. Moyes offered to sell some of his stock at the Swamp Tours. Was good for the tourists, and of course, he and his partner Jesse are doing right by it."

"Doesn't explain why Mr. Aberdeen is sweet on you. Forgive the pun."

"Oh." Eugenie started fanning herself. "He found out that I was interested in his wares. I think he wanted to find out if I could be interested in him."

"So, what did you say? Yes? No? Take a hike?"

"Well, Miss Roxie. You know I am a lady, but I am also a woman. I said yes, of course."

"Well, ain't that a lagniappe. This calls for a celebration. Nothing better than a—"

"Doberge Cake?"

"Great minds think alike."

"Bien sur, sha."

Chapter Fifty-Nine - Cleanup

And God looked down upon the special part of His vineyard. He determined it needed a good cleaning. So, He sent the East Wind. The heavens opened, and it rained and rained and washed away the traces of Death. He saw that the people and their bayou had peace once again.

And God was well-pleased.

Made in the
USA
Middletown, DE